D0285656

KIDSBORO

Kidsboro

Battle for Control
The Rise and Fall of the Kidsborian Empire
The Creek War
The Risky Reunion

FOCUS ON THE FAMILY®

The Creek War

by Marshal Younger

from Adventures in Odyssey®

Tyndale House Publishers, Inc.
Carol Stream, Illinois

A Focus on the Family book published by
Tyndale House Publishers, Inc., Carol Stream, Illinois 60188

Editor: Kathy Davis
Cover design by Joseph Sapulich
Cover illustration © 2008 by Rob Johnson. All rights reserved.

Library of Congress Cataloging-in-Publication Data
Younger, Marshal.
The Creek War / Marshal Younger.
p. cm. — (Kidsboro ; 3) (Adventures in Odyssey)
Summary: Ryan Cummings, mayor of Kidsboro, leads his town to war against Max Darby's Bettertown, in this story about loyalty, forgiveness, and learning to live together in peace.
ISBN-13: 978-1-58997-411-1
ISBN-10: 1-58997-411-5
[1. War—Fiction. 2. Conduct of life—Fiction. 3. Christian life—Fiction.] I. Title.
PZ7.Y8943Cr 2008
[Fic]—dc22

2007009163

Printed in the United States of America
1 2 3 4 5 6 7 8 9 /13 12 11 10 09 08

For Paityn,
my second-born,
who smiles for no reason,
except to make my day.

• • •

ONE

POETIC JUSTICE

I SAT AND WATCHED Max squirm in his chair. For him, every second was more painful than the one before. I wished I could videotape the moment and watch it over and over at home, and maybe invite people over to have a "watch Max squirm" party. But I was told I couldn't bring a camera into the courtroom.

"Guilty!" Pete, the prosecuting attorney, shouted, banging his hand on the table. He winced a little bit. Clearly he had hurt himself, but knowing the jury was watching, he clenched his teeth and went on. "That is the perfect word to describe Max Darby—not just today but throughout his entire life. He has been guilty of so many crimes within the walls of this town that it would be impossible to count them. But in this court case, right here, today, we're going to attempt to do just that—count how many people have been ripped off by Max Darby."

The jury was visibly nodding, as well as everyone else in the jam-packed meeting hall pavilion, which doubled as our courtroom. Max sat at the defendant's table, nervously tapping his pencil on his knuckles. He had on his best suit and his favorite cowboy boots. I think he felt the boots made him look more rural and, therefore, more friendly. But today they made him seem like a dishonest used-car salesman who wanted you to *believe* he was friendly.

It was obvious he knew the end was near. Twenty-nine people had shown up to watch Max get trounced—the entire population of Kidsboro. As for me, Ryan Cummings, mayor of Kidsboro, I couldn't have been happier.

I reclined in my chair and prepared for an entertaining show. This was something I'd anticipated for a long time. Max Darby had burned so many people with so many tricks that I doubted he had a friend left in all of Kidsboro. For nine months I had tried to get him thrown out of town, but he always had some legal loophole that made him technically innocent of his scams. Plus, the city council—made up of the five original members of Kidsboro, myself included—had always been afraid to throw him out because his father owned a construction company, and Max had access to large amounts of wood—the wood with which we built our clubhouses. But now our hesitation to throw him out was over. A boy named Mark had become a citizen during the summer, and he'd shown us all how to make clubhouses out of tarp—so we didn't need Max's wood anymore.

After that, I had led an effort to throw Max out. I contacted all of the people who had ever been cheated by Max and asked them to testify at a trial. Legally, I figured Max had a technicality to stand on for every scheme he pulled, but put them all together and a jury might decide to throw the book at him. After I had a list of people who would testify, I just waited for Max to strike again—and he did.

This is what the trial was about: Max had bought a plot of land on the shore of the creek and had built very nice, two-story clubhouses on it. Each was furnished with a bed, chairs, and even a recliner that Nelson, our town inventor, had made for him. The nicest feature, though, was siding. None of the other clubhouses in Kidsboro had siding, and I had to admit, it looked really sharp. Most of our walls were slabs of uneven wood boards. But the siding in Max's clubhouses made the new models look almost like real houses. Max sold two of these houses to citizens of Kidsboro. Little did they know that the siding was made out of painted cardboard. The first time it rained the roofs sagged in and large pieces of siding drooped and fell off the houses. It was a classic Max scheme. So the owners of the houses were now suing, with Pete as their lawyer.

"The defendant, Mr. Max Darby," Pete said, "is going to come up here and tell you that the people he sold houses to bought them *knowing* that their siding was made out of cardboard. After all, it's in the contract, and since these people signed the contract stating that they had read through the entire thing, they must have known. Ladies and gentlemen of the jury, he is telling the truth. Technically, Max is right in saying that the fact that the siding was made out of cardboard is, indeed, in the contract. But let's have a look at this contract."

Pete walked quickly to his table and grabbed a thick stack of papers. He held it up for the jury to see and slammed it back down on the table. The legs wobbled and the people in the front row jumped back. "This is the contract: 38 single-spaced pages of impossible reading material. Legal jargon, 14-letter words, and enough Latin to choke a Trojan horse. Allow me to read an excerpt from page 16: '*Pluribus equus caput capitis es horridus plebeius.*' Translated from Latin this very loosely means: 'Many horse heads are scary and uneducated.' The point I'm trying to make here is that none of this contract makes sense. It's just thousands and thousands of words thrown together for the purpose of boring the reader out of his mind. There are very few people in the world who would be willing to read through the entire thing."

The jury was smiling at the Latin translation. Pete went on. "And why, you ask, does Max not want you to read the entire thing? Let me read an excerpt from this contract, buried on page 27, in the middle of a 573-word paragraph. It reads, and I quote: 'Without limiting the generality of the foregoing, the party of the second part, hereafter referred to as The Seller, will indemnify the non-excepted payments. The siding is made out of cardboard. Whenever any claim or demand is instituted in order to defray expenses . . .' " Pete's voice trailed off. He'd made his point.

"So, yes, the siding material is in the contract. But you and I both know that Max had no intention of anyone actually reading through this entire contract to get to that one fact. It's a scheme—a scheme that we all know too well. For this case, I will parade witness after witness before you to show you a pattern of this type of behavior. You will be amazed at how many people in this community have been ripped off by Max Darby."

One by one, Pete called witnesses up to the stand to testify how Max had tricked them out of their money or property. And every time someone stepped down, Max sank a little bit lower in his seat.

Then, as if wanting to go out on his own terms, he suddenly flew up in the middle of someone's testimony and yelled, "Forget it! No more of this! This is ridiculous, and I don't even care! I don't need this town! You guys are a bunch of whining little twirps, and I'm sick of being a citizen here." I guess he had given up on trying to appear friendly. "Don't bother kicking me out. I quit!" He stormed out.

Nobody was quite sure what to do at this point. Pete had six more witnesses that he was ready to call to the stand, plus he had a closing argument I'm sure he was dying to wow the jury with. He turned to Judge Amy, who probably thought she ought to rule something. But did she need to rule anything? Pete and I exchanged looks, and then Amy shrugged her shoulders and lifted her gavel.

"Court's adjourned," she said, pounding the gavel on the table. Everyone sat silently for a moment, and then I heard someone snickering. It was Scott Sanchez, my best friend and one of the many who'd been tricked by Max before. Suddenly, he let out a burst of joyful laughter, followed by the laughter of others. People around him started clapping, including me, and soon everyone in the assembly hall was smiling and giggling and high-fiving each other. The place was oozing with joy. We had rid the evil king! We had bested the giant troll! Ding dong, the witch was dead! Kidsboro was free at last!

It was a revival of sorts, but as it turned out, it was a short-lived one. For at that moment, no one could have dreamed of what Max would do for revenge.

TWO

THE COMPETITION

THE GRASS CRUNCHED UNDER my feet, evidence of the first frost of the year. It was a weekend morning in late October. Cold weather came early in Odyssey. I was on my way to a city council meeting where we would discuss who would replace Max and become our newest citizen. The Kidsboro city charter stated that whenever someone left the city, a new person could immediately be brought in to fill the spot. There was a small problem involved with this situation, however. Max had built an incredible six-room clubhouse, the largest house in Kidsboro. It didn't seem fair that a brand-new citizen would be able to move into his home. There were people who had been in Kidsboro since the beginning who still owned only small, one-room clubhouses. So this meeting was also about who would get Max's house.

The five members of the city council were at the meeting hall pavilion promptly, though not all of them were fully awake. Scott let out an enormous yawn. "Good morning, Scott," I said.

He mumbled back, "Morning, Ryan." His dark hair was

sticking up out of the side of his head in an involuntary ponytail.

Jill Segler came in with a soda, knowing full well it was a questionable health choice, but justifying herself by saying, "All journalists have caffeine in the morning, and I'm not into coffee yet."

Police Chief Alice Funderburk was in her warm-up suit, leaning against a pole. The pole and the section of roof held up by it appeared to be ready to collapse under the weight of Alice. She was the only one who looked awake. I figured she had been up for over two hours already, lifting weights and jogging her usual two miles before breakfast.

Nelson Swanson was dazed, and I couldn't tell if he was trying to wake up, or if he was in that little world of his where he hears nothing and sees nothing around him. He was usually in this state when he was dreaming up a new invention. His glasses had a big white stain in the middle of one lens, and I couldn't imagine how he could see through it. He didn't seem to notice.

I sat down and opened a notebook that contained a list of possible candidates to take Max's place.

"Anybody got a name that sticks out?" I asked. They acted as if they hadn't heard me. The silence was broken by a distant hammering. I seemed to be the only one intrigued by the question of who would be hammering in Kidsboro this early in the morning. I scanned the main road of the town and saw no one. Ignoring the noise, I went back to my list.

"How about Monica Sertich? She's pretty nice." Silence. Scott's face wrinkled up as though he was trying to remember who Monica Sertich was, even though I knew that he'd known her for eight years. Alice was the only one who wasn't dazed, but she very rarely voiced an opinion about anything. The hammering stopped, and a power drill started up.

I was much too curious to stay in the pavilion with my catatonic friends. Alice followed me, apparently curious as well. The noise was coming from a strange distance. It was too far away to have been anywhere in Kidsboro, yet it wasn't far enough to be construction on a real house. Alice and I strolled farther and farther without a word, and the drilling gave way to hammering again. A few steps more, and we could hear voices. The hammering was now doubled, as if someone were helping. We both saw it at the same time. There, across the creek, were Max and a friend, building a clubhouse. I moved in to get a closer look.

"What are you doing, Max?" I called.

He smiled and gave a half-salute. "Howdy, neighbor."

"What's going on?"

"Just building me a house," he said in his Southern accent, an accent that came and went as he pleased.

"Why?"

"Well, since I can't live in Kidsboro anymore, I figured I'd start my own little town." Alice and I exchanged looks.

"Your own town?" I asked.

"Sure. This isn't Kidsboro property over here across the creek. I didn't think anybody'd mind if I just settled right here. Hey, a little later on, I'm gonna need some help moving my house over here from Kidsboro. You think you could help out?"

"That's not your house anymore, Max," I said.

"Oh, I beg to differ," he said with a smile. "I built that house myself. It's a nice one too. I wouldn't dream of leaving it behind."

"You want me to take him out?" Alice whispered, feeling her right hip as if she wished she had a weapon there. I didn't encourage her.

I was desperate for an ingenious reply to Max, but all I came up with was, "You can't do this."

His more-than-adequate reply: "Why not?"

In my mind, I scrambled for any reason. As far as I knew, he was right—the Kidsboro property line stopped at the creek, so if he wanted to start his own town, he was perfectly within his rights to do so. And he did build the house himself with his own materials, so he could do whatever he wanted with it.

The three other members of the city council joined us and stared across the creek at Max as well.

"What is *he* doing?" Scott asked.

"He's starting his own town."

Scott was offended. "He can't do that!"

"Why not?" I asked.

"Because he's . . . He can't just . . . It's got to be in the city charter somewhere."

"The Kidsboro city limits end at the creek, Scott," I said. "As long as he's not on Kidsboro property, Max doesn't have to pay any attention to our laws."

Nelson shook his head. "This is not good."

"No kidding," Scott replied.

"No telling what kind of town it's gonna be. And the

citizens? Probably the dregs of society—ignoring all the laws and constantly harassing us. It'll be like living near one of those high-crime suburbs that nobody likes to talk about."

"Are they out of my jurisdiction if they commit a crime over there?" Alice asked.

"I wonder how he plans to destroy us," Jill said, taking out her reporter's notebook and jotting something down.

"Listen," I began, "maybe he was . . . just unsatisfied with the way we ran things over here, so he's exercising his constitutional right to secede from the union and create his own state."

Jill stepped toward the creek. "Hey, Max!" she called.

"Yeah?"

"What's the name of your new city?"

"Bettertown," he said, smiling. Everybody looked at me and raised their eyebrows. I think they all knew, and I suppose *I* knew deep down in my heart, that we had a fight on our hands.

• • •

I left Kidsboro without any more thought to our scheduled city council meeting and headed to Whit's End, Odyssey's ice cream shop and discovery emporium. I was certain that Mr. Whittaker, the owner and operator of the place and the founder of Kidsboro, would have something to say about Max starting his own town. Mr. Whittaker owned the woods behind Whit's End, where both Kidsboro and Bettertown were situated. If he said Max had to go, his word would be final.

Before I even sat down at the counter, I was already into

my story. "Max is starting his own town!" I said to Mr. Whittaker.

"I know."

"He's across the creek, building a . . . what?"

"I know, Ryan," Mr. Whittaker said. "He was in here last night and asked permission." My face burned. This was typical Max. He was always a step ahead of everyone else.

"And you said yes?" I asked weakly.

"I didn't see any reason why not."

"But . . . don't you know Max? The only reason he's building this town is to tear ours down! He just wants to get even because we forced him out. His only purpose is to destroy Kidsboro!"

"Oh, I don't think there's really anything Max could do to destroy Kidsboro. I'm actually thinking it could be good for you."

"What?"

"Healthy competition. I'm sure he'll create new businesses. It'll force your business owners to make better products and lower prices so that they can compete with Max's businesses. It'll give you a taste of the real world."

I didn't want a taste of the real world. I was very happy in my imaginary one, a world that for about 12 hours didn't include Max. "He doesn't want healthy competition, Mr. Whittaker."

"Ryan, I know Max. I know what he's like. I know he's schemed his way to the top, and if things go the way they usually do, he'll scheme his way back to the bottom. But I also know that there's hardly anyone more capable of being the leader of a town that could compete with Kidsboro. He's smart, he's ambitious, and he knows how to get things done. I wouldn't do this unless I thought it would be good for you. Who knows? Just like different countries of the world, you may end up needing each other."

"I'm sorry for saying so, Mr. Whittaker, but I can't imagine this being good for us."

"I guess you'll soon see."

I walked out the door of Whit's End, my shoulders drooping. I reached down, picked up a rock, and threw it at a tree. How could Mr. Whittaker show no loyalty to Kidsboro? The town was his idea. He had helped write the laws and set up the government. And now he was going to let it be taken over. I couldn't understand it.

• • •

For the next month, we could barely hear ourselves think with all the construction going on in Max's new town. Eight of his friends were working, and, from the looks of it, not all of the structures they were building were houses. Max was mum on what he was creating, which had Jill fuming, of course. She had tried to interview him a number of times, but he kept answering questions such as, "What kinds of things will you have in your town?" with comebacks like, "Good things." The construction workers didn't know anything either—they were just following orders.

I was watching them work on an odd-shaped, three-story building (I'm not sure I would have the guts to go up to the third story) when Nelson came up from behind me.

"Look at this," he said, handing me a piece of paper. It was a flyer.

GRAND OPENING!!!

BETTERTOWN
COME SEE THE ATTRACTIONS! EAT THE FOOD!
LIVE THE EXCITEMENT! ALL FOR FREE! ALL FOR FUN!
THE DAY AFTER THANKSGIVING

"Our location is just across the creek,
but our attitude is miles away."
Sponsored by Max Darby, King of Bettertown

Nelson watched my reaction as I read it. "These flyers are all over Odyssey. I guess he's inviting pretty much anyone," he said.

I decided right then and there that this was going to be for real, and I could not show others that I was scared of it. People were going to look to me for leadership, and I had to convince them with my actions that I was not threatened by Max's new town.

I swallowed and said unconvincingly, "Good. I'm looking forward to going."

"You're going?"

"Sure. They're our new neighbors. We need to be neighborly."

"This town is obviously a direct attempt to bring us down. I mean, look at their slogan. 'Our attitude is miles away.' That's a slam on Kidsboro, and you know it."

"There's nothing like competitive juices to stimulate people."

Of course, I was unable to look Nelson in the eye when I said that.

• • •

Jill, Scott, and I went to the grand opening together. I encouraged everyone in town to go, though I didn't really have to twist anyone's arm. Max had done well to keep everything secret, and now people were brimming with anticipation. Plus, there was free food.

Max had spared no expense getting his town ready. There were flags, balloons, and streamers everywhere. The smell of barbecue was in the air, music was playing, and in every direction there was a beehive of activity. Max was decked out in a shirt and tie (one of those string ties that country singers wear) and dress slacks, greeting everyone with a welcome smile as they came across the bridge to Bettertown. I think mine was more of a welcome sneer.

The first thing I noticed was the housing district. It was the Beverly Hills of the woods. Two-story clubhouses were lined up, majestically overlooking the creek. They all had "For Sale" signs hanging on posts in the front yards. The three of us went into one of the houses, and Jill almost choked on her tongue. Smooth, painted walls and ceilings, plywood floors (the floors in Kidsboro were dirt), and two soft chairs decorated the first floor. A ladder led up to the second floor where there was a 10-foot cathedral ceiling, a small balcony, and—most impressive to Scott and me—electricity. Max had put outlets in each of the houses. They were connected to mammoth extension cords, which disappeared underground outside the houses. He had dug a trench from the town and wired the cords through a pipe under the bridge, through Kidsboro, and all the way to Whit's End.

I wondered if Mr. Whittaker had helped Max just as he had helped us build Kidsboro. Kidsboro had electrical access, with the same underground cables, but it was only hooked up in certain places like the meeting hall and the movie theater. If Mr. Whittaker had helped Max out, that meant he had gone to greater lengths to help Bettertown than he had to help Kidsboro. My teeth clenched as I bent down to look at the trench.

Mr. Whittaker's work, I was sure of it.

Max had proudly placed an electric appliance in each of the houses—a radio, a fan, a CD player—to demonstrate the possibilities with a house hooked up to electricity. Scott was mesmerized by the working radio, as if he'd never seen one before. "Excuse me for saying so, but this is awesome."

Jill was enchanted by the balcony and the painted walls. I tried to act like it was nothing special, but to be honest, I was impressed.

The business district was no less impressive. The crowd seemed to be flocking to a large meeting area inland. It was a building much larger than the meeting pavilion in Kidsboro, and it turned out to be a hangout. There was a sign on the door that said "Max's Room." We rolled our eyes as we went in. Tables and chairs were set up. People were mingling and eating popcorn and chips and drinking sodas. There was a concession stand with a line of people waiting to get free food.

The front four tables were arranged so that people could watch Charlie Metzger, a boy from Odyssey Middle School, perform magic tricks on a stage that was raised about six inches off the ground. To his left was a large, white poster board on an easel with the schedule of performances for the day. "Jim Jones, the Junior High Juggler" would perform at noon.

At one o'clock, "The Vocal Stylings of Margaret Piloscowitz" was scheduled. So she was either a singer, or she made funny noises. I probably wouldn't attend in either case.

At two o'clock, Slugfest, an alternative band from our school that consisted of four electric guitars and a guy who played a tambourine and sang every now and then, was playing. The school newspaper had done a story on them once. The reporter had asked them why their songs didn't rhyme, make sense, or contain any complete sentences. The guy with the tambourine had answered that it was because *life* didn't rhyme, make sense, or contain complete sentences. I asked around, and nobody knew what that meant, but everyone thought it was a totally cool thing to say.

Then at three o'clock was "The Rip-Roaring Comedy of Herb Martin." Herb had done a comedy act at a school talent show once and he wasn't funny, but he could pop any joint in his body at will. His routine was pretty much centered around this talent.

"We gotta come back at three," Scott said. "Herb Martin is hilarious."

Jill seemed hesitant to say anything complimentary, probably fearing she'd hurt my feelings. But she did note, "Interesting place."

"It's great," I said, stating the obvious. If I'd said, "This is five times better than anything we have in Kidsboro," that would've been a little more accurate.

Charlie the magician pulled a yardstick out of his hat, and the trick was met with a decent amount of applause. He bowed and said, "Thank you! I'll be here throughout the holidays. Also, if you'd like to learn how to be a magician yourself, starting December third I'll be teaching a class called 'Beginning Magic' at the Bettertown Community School. Thank you."

Jill and I looked at each other. "They have a school?"

• • •

The school wasn't nearly as nice as anything else we had seen, probably because Max had run out of his seemingly endless supply of wood. The classrooms were divided up by bed sheets hanging from the trees. Each classroom had blankets for the pupils to sit on, and a desk and blackboard for the teacher. There was no ceiling.

"Education always gets the least amount of money, huh?" Jill said, her political commentary for the day.

Outside of the school, a table was set up with a list of the classes that would be offered. A girl I had never seen before was behind the table, taking applications and answering questions. I looked at the list of subjects: Beginning Magic, Bowling, Extreme Sports, Basic Guitar, Wizards and Warlocks (a popular card game that our school had banned because of its references to the occult), Juggling, and a class titled, "Figuring Out Girls." There was a note informing us that more classes would be offered at a later date.

Next to the class names were the names of the teachers of each. I didn't recognize some of the names, but Charlie Metzger was going to teach magic, Jim Jones juggling, one of the members of Slugfest was to teach guitar, and Paul Isringhausen, the Odyssey teen bowling champ, was going to teach bowling. I couldn't believe that Max actually got Paul Isringhausen to teach a class. He was practically a celebrity.

"Figuring Out Girls" was going to be taught by Ted Russo, a junior who had dated 6 of the 10 most beautiful girls at Odyssey High School (according to an informal poll taken by the football team). He was one of the most popular guys in the school. How did Max, a middle schooler, get someone like Ted to come to his little clubhouse town in the woods?

When I asked Jill this question, she gave me an immediate answer. "*That's* how he got those guys to teach," she said, pointing to a small building that looked like a photo booth. The sign said, "Money Exchange," and it was a place where you could exchange real money for the currency used in Bettertown. There was no one in the building, probably because everything was free this day, so no one needed any Bettertown money. I looked inside, and posted on the back wall was the exchange rate: the number of "darbles" you could get for a dollar. Jill and I exchanged another roll of the eyes, noting that Max had again named something after himself ("darbles": Darby).

"You see," Jill said, "he's making money off of tourists coming in, so he can get outside people to teach by offering them real money."

Across from each teacher's name was how much the class would cost. The bowling class was $15 for non-residents of Bettertown and 400 darbles for residents. The "Figuring Out Girls" class was about the same. They were easily the most expensive ones. It appeared that Jill was right.

• • •

We were weaving our way through the quickly thickening crowd when I saw Sid staring into space, kneading his hands like he was washing them with imaginary soap. Sid owned Sid's Bakery in Kidsboro and was a master chef.

"What's the matter?" I asked him.

He didn't say a word, only pointed his chin slightly forward. We all looked and saw a store with a sign that said "Le Bakeria." It was a full-service bakery. Sid looked at me and shook his head. I assured him that no one could beat his donuts, and he said he knew that. But these appeared to be cheaper (apparently he had already calculated how many of our tokens would equal a darble), and most kids didn't care about the quality of their food. So he figured he was in trouble.

Scott stepped forward, obviously wanting to taste one since they were free, but he looked at Sid and, out of loyalty, did not grab one. Jill tried to make Sid feel better by saying that the words *Le Bakeria* were not French or Spanish or anything for bakery, but Sid was inconsolable.

There were a few more businesses that seemed to be

mirror images of attractions in Kidsboro, only claiming to be of higher quality or having lower prices. Mark, the owner and operator of the miniature golf place in Kidsboro, had the same reaction that Sid had to the bakery when he laid his eyes on the Bettertown recreation center. This indoor/outdoor facility had an arcade-like area with carnival games like basketball pop-a-shot and football throw, two dart boards, an archery range, a weight bench, and an outdoor bowling alley with three lanes. Mark was not pleased. I had been repeating Mr. Whittaker's words and telling everyone that the competition would be good for us. I'm not sure getting blown away by your competition is all that good for anyone.

• • •

On our way back to the bridge, we passed a table set up with applications for Bettertown citizenship. There was an illustrated brochure showing all the highlights. It looked like something from Disney World. So far, Bettertown was exactly what its name implied. In every conceivable way, it made Kidsboro look pitiful. I was starting to feel a little sorry for myself.

On our way over the bridge, we met Mr. Whittaker, who was heading over to Bettertown. He caught my eye, and I quickly looked away. My reaction was too obvious, though, so I looked at him again. He smiled at me, and I tried to smile back.

"Hi, Ryan," he said.

"Hi, Mr. Whittaker." We passed each other with nothing to say. I didn't want to feel this way about Mr. Whittaker, but I couldn't help it. I felt the knife in my back.

THREE

THE BETTERTOWN ADVANTAGE

THE ONE SAVING GRACE in all of this was that I couldn't imagine how Max was going to get anyone to live in his town. I figured tourists would flock to Bettertown because of all of its attractions. People might even go to school there since some interesting classes were being offered. But who would live in those houses? I knew Max would charge an arm and a leg for them. Plus, knowing his greedy nature, I figured that the prices of everything else would be high too. But the main disadvantage was this: What would it be like to live in a place where Max had proclaimed himself king? Everyone knew he was a con artist. Who would voluntarily live in a place where he made the laws?

After school on Monday, I grabbed my copy of the *Kidsboro Chronicle* off the ground and went to Scott's clubhouse. I skimmed through the paper on the way. The entire newspaper was dedicated to the opening of Bettertown. Jill had written most of the stories, including a full-page interview with Max, an in-depth article about all of the attractions, and a story about the school. Roberto, Jill's assistant, had taken photographs and written a few articles himself. According to the statistics on page three, 104 people had passed over the bridge to attend the grand opening, and two had applied for citizenship. It was exactly as I'd expected—everyone wanted to visit, but no one wanted to live there.

Scott was reading a comic book when I went into his house. His eyes focused on my newspaper the second I passed through the door. "Oh, let me see your paper," he said, snatching it from me. He looked with great interest at the front page.

"The whole thing is about Bettertown," I said. "The grand opening was a huge success. Of course, Max is having a hard time getting people to live there."

"Yeah, I bet," Scott said, with an unnatural chuckle.

As he read on, lips moving, I glanced at his desk and noticed a Bettertown brochure. I hadn't seen Scott pick one up when we were there, so I wondered if he went back for it. I lifted it, and Scott looked horrified.

"I, uh," he stumbled, "I didn't . . . somebody gave that to me. I was going to throw it away."

He saw my face and must have sensed a look of disapproval. I tried to hide it. "It's okay, Scott. Go ahead and be curious. *I* am. And don't worry about going over, spending time there, whatever. It's a fun place. I'm even thinking of taking a class at the school. I've always wanted to learn how to do magic tricks." Actually, the thought *had* crossed my mind to learn magic, but I was hesitant to spend even one dime in Bettertown. Far be it from me to help their economy.

Scott's shoulders were still tense, as though he felt no relief that I wasn't mad at him. He stared at me like he expected me to do something, and then opened the newspaper back up.

I glanced through the brochure, and then I noticed something on the back page of the newspaper. I sat down on the opposite side of the desk and read it while Scott read a page in the middle.

It was a full-page advertisement, paid for by Max. It read:

Are you tired of being a lower-class citizen?
Living in a run-down clubhouse?
Having trouble making ends meet?
THEN BE A CITIZEN OF
***** **BETTERTOWN** *****
WHERE
EVERYONE IS RICH!!!
Come to an informational meeting at the meeting hall in Bettertown
5:30 P.M. Tuesday night
See a multimedia presentation about
THE TOWN OF THE FUTURE
*****BETTERTOWN*****
PAID FOR BY KING MAX I OF BETTERTOWN

The first thing that struck me was the appeal to the lower class—the people who didn't have much money to spend. Kidsboro did sort of have a lower class, though there weren't too many people in it. These were the people who had trouble finding work for themselves. They didn't have their own businesses, or if they did, their businesses weren't very profitable. These people either had to work for someone else, or they had to get by on small incomes.

Kidsboro had had an economic boom the summer before, with new businesses springing up everywhere, but these businesses could employ only a few. Scott was one of the people who didn't have a real job. He ran a detective agency, but he had only investigated two cases since we'd started Kidsboro eleven months earlier. Other jobs had come and gone, but Scott usually had no money. He also made poor choices about spending what money he did have. I guess you could say he was part of the Kidsboro lower class.

But how would Max eliminate the lower class? What did he mean by saying that everyone would be rich? That was impossible. How in the world did he think he would get people to believe this?

Something told me that I needed to show up at this meeting.

• • •

Obviously, I didn't want anyone to see me at the meeting. Max would think I was spying and change his presentation. I wanted to hear it just as it was, with no editing. I looked at the advertisement again, and noticed that it was going to be a multimedia presentation. I had seen Max's computer presentations before, and the lights were always turned off. I figured I would wait until the lights were down, and then sneak in and watch from the back. I would sneak out before the lights went back up.

I went in just as someone turned the lights down, and I peered around the room. I couldn't make out many of the faces, but I could see silhouettes . . . lots of them. The place was packed! Max moved to his computer and began typing things in. His presentation began.

A thundering *boom!* shook the whole building, and everybody jumped in their seats. It was followed by embarrassed laughter. Fireworks filled the screen, and red, white, and blue letters swooped down from the upper right and, with majestic fanfare, spelled out "BETTERTOWN." Max's voice echoed, saying, "Bettertown. The town of the future."

Very impressive.

After a lot more of the echoing stuff, a short video came on. On-screen, Edward, a boy from Odyssey Middle School, came out of his Bettertown creek-view house. Edward was a loner. He didn't have many friends at school. In fact, he sat alone at lunch every day. I always thought it was kind of sad, and that if I ever had the same lunch period he did, I would sit next to him.

But here he was in Max's video. I couldn't believe Max got him to do it. Edward didn't seem to be the dramatic type.

Then Valerie Swanson came on-screen. Valerie was Nelson's sister and a citizen of Kidsboro, though not a very loyal one. It didn't surprise me that she was doing a video for Max. Valerie will be a shoo-in for the football team's annual "Most Beautiful Girls" poll when she gets to high school. She'll probably take the top spot as a freshman and hold onto it until she graduates. She flipped her long, brown hair away from her face as she turned toward Edward. Max must have paid her an awful lot to get her to be in this video with him.

Edward awkwardly looked past the camera, as if a director was behind it urging him to say his line. He cleared his throat and began, "Hi, Honey."

"Hi, Sweetie," Valerie said, and they patted each other on the back.

This was beyond unrealistic. This was science fiction. Edward and Valerie?

A girl I didn't recognize came on-screen looking surprised. "Joe? Is that you?"

Edward looked surprised that someone called him "Joe." His name was, in fact, Edward. Edward glanced toward the director again, and then said to the girl, "Yes. Is that you, Marcia?"

"Yes. I can't believe it. Are you and Grace together?"

Valerie smiled and flipped her hair back again. "That's right, Marcia. Joe and I are a couple." That line alone had probably cost Max 30 bucks.

"Wow, Joe," Marcia said. "You used to be such a geek. What happened?"

"I'll tell you what happened, Tara . . . I mean, Marcia," Edward said. "I became a citizen of Bettertown."

"Really?" Marcia said. "So did I." Then she went on about how she had been broke, hungry, and lying in the gutter when Max Darby came along and told her about Bettertown. Now she had a house with a balcony, she was continuing her education at the Bettertown Community School (to be a juggler, maybe?), and she felt like she had a future.

Then Edward smiled at Valerie and said, "I used to be the laughingstock of my school. But now, I'm the envy. In fact, I've got the entire eighth-grade class coming over for a barbecue tomorrow. I'm so thankful for Bettertown."

Then they both looked into the camera, and, with big cheesy smiles, they said in unison, "Thanks, King Max."

Finally, the real message of the presentation came on: the explanation of how Bettertown would work, how there were no social classes, and how everyone was equal.

Max's voice narrated, accompanied by words flying onto the screen in different colors and fonts.

The gist of it was this: Everyone would get a *free* house. The house would be owned by the city, but no one would pay rent. Everyone would work in Bettertown—whether at the bakery, the recreation center, the school, or wherever—for the exact same wage. No one received more for doing a harder or more complicated job. This way, there would be no class system, no low-income people, and everyone would be a team.

At the end of the presentation, a magnificent shot of the creek filled the background, and the flag of Bettertown—five red stick figures holding hands as a show of unity, with a green star above them (probably representing Max, though he didn't say it)—dissolved up into the foreground. The music stopped.

I quickly stood up and reached for the door. Nobody had seen me. But before I could get out, the lights came back on, and I saw a few of the people inside. And just before I closed the door, I saw something I couldn't believe. Sitting in the front of the meeting room, with a pen and paper . . . was Scott.

FOUR

BETRAYAL

I WANTED TO GIVE Scott the benefit of the doubt. Maybe he was there for the same reason I was there—to find out what Max was up to. Maybe he was just curious. But he had seemed awfully guilty when I'd found that brochure in his clubhouse. And why would he have a pen and paper with him, apparently taking notes?

I met Nelson at Whit's End, and I told him about the meeting. He called Eugene Meltsner over. Eugene was a college student and Odyssey's resident genius. Nelson and I told him about Bettertown's economic system.

"That's communism," Eugene said, pushing his glasses up on the bridge of his nose. "Or at least a rudimentary version of it. It is based on the notion that there's no such thing as personal property. Everything is owned by the government, and everyone is paid exactly what they need, no more, no less. It's Marxism."

I had heard of communism before, but all that I remembered was that it was a bad thing, as if people who were communists were evil.

"There's nothing wrong with communism in theory," Eugene said. "Its goal is to create a society in which the working class operates the government. But it also limits freedom. Citizens cannot own anything or start their own businesses. It opens itself up to corruption because the government officials control everything, and they can become power-hungry and start ruling for their *own* benefit, as opposed to the people's."

Nelson and I both raised our eyebrows. Max was the government, and if there was ever a leader who was capable of corruption, it was him. Bettertown and its people were doomed.

"Scott was at the meeting," I told them.

"Why? To spy?" Nelson asked.

"I don't know. I didn't know he was going to be there. But he took notes, like he was interested in it."

"In becoming a citizen?"

"I don't know."

"You gotta talk to him."

• • •

A special edition of the *Chronicle* reported that 17 people had applied for citizenship in Bettertown. I was surprised at the high number, so I went to Jill to find out who they were. She said that Max wouldn't give her specific names. I wondered how many of the 17 were Kidsborians who were defecting.

The traffic in Kidsboro was high, but it was mainly because tourists were heading through to get to Bettertown. I stopped at Sid's Bakery, and he was visibly miffed by the potential customers who passed by his store without even a whiff. Signs in front of his bakery advertised muffins. Prices had been slashed twice, from five tokens to four tokens to two tokens. Sid had a marker at the ready when I came up; apparently ready to make the muffins two for a token.

"Did you taste those donuts over there?" he asked.

"No."

"They're dry and way too sweet. Whoever bakes those things needs to take it easy on the sugar."

"Your customers will figure it out at some point, Sid."

"I'm practically giving these muffins away. I'm making no profit. I sent a spy over there an hour ago, and he hasn't come back yet. He's probably sampling their cream puffs—which, by the way, are much too flaky."

"Well, Sid, you've been the only bakery business around since we started. Now you have some competition. Maybe this'll force you to work a little harder. Present a better product. Advertise a little."

"Well, I'll tell you what. I'm not going down without a fight."

"That's the spirit!"

• • •

As I passed Le Bakeria, I got a few whiffs of something, and I was tempted to try whatever it was that smelled so good. But I couldn't do that to Sid. I noticed that there was a fan running behind the counter. Mind you, it was early December and about 40 degrees out, so the fan wasn't there for cooling purposes. It was there to send the smell wafting out to the masses, and it seemed to be working. People were being drawn like bees to pollen. Sid was going to have to do something special to get his customers back, though I didn't doubt for a second that Sid's food was better than anything they served at Le Bakeria.

I noticed a number of Kidsborians there, and when they saw me looking at them, a few ducked out of sight. Apparently, they didn't want to explain their presence in Bettertown.

But then I saw something that bothered me much more than that. I passed the recreation area, and there, resetting the bowling pins, was Scott. He didn't see me; he was busy trying to keep up with the bowlers, running from lane to lane, setting the pins back up after they were knocked down. Sweat was running down his face despite the 40 degree temperature, and he looked a little flustered.

I stood there watching, not wanting him to see me, but knowing that at some point there had to be a confrontation. Max came up from behind me.

"Good kid," he said, seeing the direction of my gaze. "Hard worker. Must be tough for you to lose him." He smiled at me, knowing how much this dug in. He left to go annoy someone else.

I walked around aimlessly for a few minutes, and then headed for the housing district. Sure enough, there was a mailbox in front of one of the houses that read "Sanchez," Scott's last name. I heard footsteps and turned. Scott froze, seeing that I had noticed the mailbox and knowing there was no rational explanation he could give for it. We stared at each other for a few moments, and then I couldn't help but speak.

"What are you doing here?"

"I'm just . . . I decided to . . . I live here," he said, looking at his shoes.

"Why?"

"I figured I needed a change of scenery. I mean, I *like* Kidsboro and all, but . . ." his eyes fixed on his house. "Well, I've only got a 10-minute break, I have to get back to work."

"What? Setting up bowling pins?"

He looked surprised and a little embarrassed that I already knew about his new profession. "Look, it's a job. At least I'm doing *something*. A lot more than I was doing over there," he said as he pointed across the creek.

"But Scott, you're working for *Max*. Don't you know he's gonna burn you?"

"He hasn't burned me yet. So far, he's given me a job, a living wage, and a house with electricity—none of which I had in Kidsboro."

"But you've got *friends* over there."

"I've got friends *here*. We had a rally yesterday, and we're a team. It's a family. I like these people."

He was making too much sense, so I resorted to a lower blow. "How could you turn on us like this? You're a charter member of Kidsboro."

"Oh, and that's really taken me far in 11 months," he said sarcastically. "You know what, Ryan?" He stepped toward me and pointed in my face. "You have no right to say that. You have no idea what it's like to be me. You're the mayor. You're the leader of the whole place. You *have* a job. You *make* a difference. Me? I'm the town fool. I have a detective agency that no one goes to, even if by some miracle they actually *have* a case to be solved. No one respects me there, Ryan. But *here*? Here, I'm a part of something. They need me. In Kidsboro, I go on vacation for two weeks and no one even knows I'm gone."

"You're on the city council in Kidsboro! You count for 20 percent of the vote."

"I'll tell you what. *You* can have my 20 percent. You pretty much had it anyway."

"What is that supposed to mean?"

"Oh, come on, Ryan. You know that whatever you voted, I voted the same. And if I didn't, you let me hear about it."

"What?"

"I mean, you always made it *sound* like you were just reasoning with me, but really you *expected* me to vote with you. You controlled me, and that's probably the problem here too. You've lost your control, and you're mad."

I was flabbergasted. "What in the world are you talking about, Scott?"

"Are you just jealous that I have a nicer house than you, Ryan? You don't think I deserve it?"

"Scott—"

"Or maybe you're having trouble dealing with the fact that there may be something over here that's better than Kidsboro. Well, for me there's no choice. In Bettertown, I'm equal with everybody else. In Kidsboro, I'm a pitiful, poor boy with a failed business and a lucky connection in city council."

He slowly dropped his finger and let out a few exasperated breaths. I caught a glimpse of a smile, like he was proud of himself for standing up to me. His resolve shocked me, and I could do nothing but drop my shoulders—and my defenses.

"Well, Scott," I said, stiffening my upper lip. "I hope you're very happy here." I walked past him.

• • •

Scott's feelings about Kidsboro troubled me. I hadn't realized that there were people in our town who were unhappy. And I'd had no idea that one of the unhappy people was my best friend. On my way back into town, I noticed Mark, the owner of the miniature golf course, playing on his own course. Well, at least he appeared to be playing, but in actuality, he was firing his shots into trees outside the course boundaries. No one else was around.

"Why would anybody play here?" he asked before he even looked at me. "There's a bowling alley over there—and darts, and archery and . . . fun. There's *fun* over there. And here? We've got a guy knocking golf balls into trees with a putter."

I told him the novelty of Bettertown would wear off, and I believed that was true, but at this point, its downfall couldn't come fast enough for me.

• • •

Usually I met with Mr. Whittaker once a week to give him an update on what was happening in Kidsboro. I wanted to meet with him this week and let him know how many problems he had caused, but I could never say that to Mr. Whittaker. Instead, I decided to avoid it completely and not meet with him at all. I went to Whit's End and was glad that he wasn't in the front. Connie Kendall was behind the counter.

"Mr. Whittaker's not here?" I asked.

"No, he's in the back. You want me to go get him?" Connie asked.

"No, could you just give him a message?"

"He's right in the back. I can get him."

"No, just a message, please. Tell him I won't be able to meet with him today."

"Well . . . okay, Ryan."

"Thanks."

• • •

I called a city council meeting to figure out what we were going to do. Pride in our town had been lost. Suddenly, no one had any reason to go to Kidsboro. We had to do something.

We started with a damage report. "We've lost six people," Jill said. This meant six Kidsborians had left and joined Bettertown. So 11 of the 17 new citizens were from elsewhere. We decided to wait to fill up those empty houses, since none of us believed that Bettertown would stand for long. At least, that's what we hoped.

"Since Bettertown's grand opening a week ago, Kidsboro businesses are down in profits by 65 percent," Nelson continued with the bad news. "Sid's Bakery has taken the biggest hit."

"The crime rate's about the same," Alice said proudly, as if Kidsboro had crime, much less a rate to keep track of.

We briefly discussed the ramifications of losing one member of the city council, and we decided we had to fill the spot. Since having a voting group of four members would result in a lot of ties, we needed a tie-breaker. But this was not first on our agenda. We had to come up with a way to drum up new interest in our city.

"Let's have a 'Pride in Kidsboro' day," Jill declared. "Like a Fourth of July thing, where everybody celebrates the country."

"That sounds great," I said. "Tell us more." The rest of the council members sat up in their chairs and took notice. Jill began slowly, giving us her ideas, then Nelson added a few of his own, and, as if new life had been breathed into us, it became an incredible brainstorming session with fresh and exciting things to add to our celebration.

By the end of the meeting, we had come up with some pretty interesting ideas. Jill was going to do a *History of Kidsboro* collector's book, outlining how Kidsboro came to be and events that had shaped Kidsboro along the way. Nelson suggested that Jill include a short biography of every citizen who had ever settled here. He reasoned that people would be more apt to buy the book if they could see their own names in print.

We were also going to have refreshments. We all agreed to bring food from home, plus, we would ask Sid to offer his cooking expertise and make a smorgasbord of pastries especially for the event. (As it turned out, Sid agreed to make the pastries and sell them for half price, but our end of the deal was that we had to advertise his bakery as much as was humanly possible. Sid was a hard sell.)

We also decided to create a flag, though admittedly, it wasn't an original idea. The Bettertown flag flew high across the creek, in full view from Kidsboro. Jill suggested that we ask Roberto to come up with some ideas because he was a pretty good artist. I told her that we needed something that symbolized what Kidsboro was all about—freedom, loyalty, peace, justice, responsibility, fun—and she said that to get all those things into one flag, we would have to fly a copy of our city charter on a pole. I told her that if he got any two of those things on the flag, I'd be happy. She said she would talk to Roberto.

Alice said that she would take care of security, "just in case things get out of hand." We all knew that things rarely got out of hand, but we nodded to support Alice's one and only contribution to the meeting.

But the one idea that we all got excited about came from Nelson.

"I've got a new invention I've been looking forward to unveiling. Eugene and I are almost done. Maybe I could do it at this thing."

"A new invention?" I said.

"Yeah. We've been working on it for about a month now, and I think we've got it just about right."

"What is it?" Jill asked.

"It's . . . in the entertainment field," he said.

Nelson's inventions were always extremely popular. Everyone loved the idea of playing with something that no one else in the world had. His last invention, a computer-programmable car, had sold 51 units in only three months. The fact that he had a new creation was not only a magnet to draw people to our celebration, but it was also good for Kidsboro. It would set us apart from Bettertown because we had something they didn't—ingenuity. Yes, they had a bowling alley, but we had Nelson. And he would bring Kidsboro back.

We decided that the celebration would be in four days, on December 10.

• • •

I stopped counting after it became clear that we were not going to get as big a crowd as Max's grand opening had. But it wasn't bad. After the rest of the town got word of the celebration, a few people got into it and created attractions of their own. Pete, our resident movie buff, made a short video presentation that was a reenactment of the settling of Kidsboro, 11 months before. It started out with the words "Birth of a Town" in big bold letters in the foreground, then in smaller letters, "Brought to you by Sid's Bakery." It was part of the deal.

In one scene, the boy playing me said to four people standing around, "What shall we do, my friends? We have fought oppression and slavery, and won. And now, I yearn for a land of freedom." And then I planted a flag in the ground. Not only did we not have a flag back then, but we never faced any oppression or slavery, nor do I ever remember having used the word *yearn*, and I most certainly didn't have a British accent, as this actor did. So, the facts were a little exaggerated, but it was still fun.

Speaking of the flag, Roberto came up with what I thought was a great symbol. It looked a lot like the American flag, with a blue field in the upper left hand corner, but instead of stars, there was a white silhouette of a big oak tree, and the trunk formed the vertical line of a K, for Kidsboro. The red and white stripes were the same, except the red stripes were thinner. He told me that this represented us, in that we were smaller, yes, but that we still wanted the same things that America did—freedom, peace, and so on. I thought it was pretty cool. He and Jill had printed out about 20 copies of the flag, and they were flying them all over town. And at the bottom of each flag, there was the fine print that read, "This flag sponsored by Sid's Bakery."

As predicted, many people bought the *History of Kidsboro* collector's book simply because it contained their names. The facts in it were more accurate than Pete's film, but it still sparked some controversy over who actually came up with some of the ideas for the town. The layout was sharp. Jill had scanned color photos and placed designer borders around the edges. The quality was only slightly marred by the Sid's Bakery ads on every other page.

Sid outdid himself with the food. He baked every pastry known to man—donuts, bagels, Danishes, coffee cakes, cheesecakes, pies, breads, muffins, cinnamon rolls, sweet rolls—and it was all delicious. I had forgotten what an asset Sid was to our community, but he proved himself once again.

Mark had lowered the price on rounds for the day, and his miniature golf course was packed. He'd even added two holes. On one you had to pretend you were crossing a city street with the ball. There were tiny plastic pedestrians walking across the street, and if you hit one, you got a one-stroke penalty. This was the type of ingenuity I was talking about.

But the highlight of the day was, of course, the unveiling of Nelson's new invention, which would occur near the creek. All day people were stopping to gaze at the large quilts that were covering the invention, curiosity oozing out their eyeballs. There was a sign next to it that read, "Nelson Swanson's new invention to be unveiled at three o'clock."

At 2:51, when I got there, there was already a crowd of at least 30 people gathered around the quilts. Nelson and Eugene walked up at exactly three o'clock with their chins raised in the air a little. Eugene had invented some very impressive things himself, most of them having to do with computer programs. He often helped Nelson with his more elementary inventions. Eugene's pride was more in Nelson, instead of their inventions. He took a couple of steps to the side of the quilts, letting Nelson have the spotlight.

Nelson smiled as he checked his watch. He looked up and breathed in heavily, as if trying to smell the anticipation of the crowd. It grew quiet. He glanced at Eugene, who nodded back.

"Ladies and gentlemen, for many years, this creek has been impossible to navigate with any kind of watercraft. Boats didn't work because, during most times of the year, the creek was too shallow, and a boat would scrape the bottom. But three months ago, I saw something that made me change my outlook regarding this impossible task. It was a water moccasin—skimming across the top of the water. I asked myself, 'Why couldn't we do that? Why couldn't we float on *top* of the water instead of sinking slightly below the surface?' And that is the reason I decided to create something that will revolutionize the way we view creek navigation.

"I present to you . . . the Water Moccasin 250!" Eugene jerked away the quilts to reveal something that looked like a go-cart without wheels. It had two seats, a steering column, a propeller on the underside, and four inflatable inner tubes serving as "wheels" on the bottom. There was a Sid's Bakery bumper sticker on the back. The crowd stepped closer and peered inside, and we saw two pairs of bicycle pedals attached to axles in front of both seats. It was very impressive.

Nelson, Eugene, and two other boys took the invention to the edge of the creek and placed it in the water. Nelson would be the first to try it, just to show the others that there was no risk of drowning. Without hesitation, he plopped down into the Moccasin and began pedaling. Sure enough, the craft floated on the water with no problem.

Eugene cleared his throat. "Notice the rubber bumpers on each side of the craft, so that rocks can't damage the sides." Nelson bounced a little as he maneuvered upstream. He pedaled frantically, the propeller twirling behind him, and the craft inched up the creek in slow motion. The amount of work Nelson had to do to get the thing to move that slowly didn't seem worthwhile.

"Now," Eugene said, "the craft's velocity will increase when another passenger is added."

Nelson ducked his head as he went under the bridge, and he continued upstream. The crowd cheered.

Nelson floated back downstream a few minutes later. He didn't even have to pedal as he went with the current. But one thing was certain: No one would be taking this thing any farther downstream, no matter how easy it was. There was a five-foot waterfall only 100 feet downstream from the bridge, and no one would risk the fall.

The crowd cheered again, and Nelson waved to the fans.

No one had ever gone that far upstream before because there was a tall fence put up by the city of Odyssey that prevented anyone from walking along the shore. But this watercraft would enable people to go upstream in the water. No one even knew what was up there. I knew this would be a popular attraction.

• • •

That day, Nelson gave everyone free five-minute rides. The passengers couldn't really get very far in five minutes, so this was a smart strategy. It made people want to try it the next day, when they would have to pay four tokens per ride but could go for 10 minutes. The crowds were lined up all day. Nelson was beaming the entire time, giving a history of the invention, and the history of boats, and the history of all things that floated, to people standing on shore while passengers took the Moccasin out.

At one point, I glanced across the creek and saw Max. He was watching the crowds line up to try Nelson's invention, stroking his chin as if he had a beard. Bettertown was noticeably quiet, and it appeared that the tide had turned. Kidsboro was the place to be on this day.

But I had seen that look in Max's eyes before. He was plotting something.

FIVE

THE WALL

I WAS ON THE way out of my real house, heading toward Kidsboro, when my mom stopped me. "Can I talk to you for a minute?"

I followed her into the living room, and she grabbed a cup of coffee off of the end table. The fingers that held the handle shook slightly, and the coffee jostled back and forth in the cup.

"What's the matter, Mom?" I asked.

"Sit down," she said, taking a sip and then placing the cup back on the end table. She paced back and forth.

"It's your father. He may be looking for us."

When I was eight years old, my mother and I left our house in California in the middle of the night to escape my abusive, alcoholic father. An abuse center helped us start our lives over. We changed our names and moved to Odyssey, where we'd been ever since. We didn't tell anyone in California where we'd gone. My father was a dangerous, violent man, and we knew that when he discovered we were gone, he would be furious.

For several years now, we had been able to hide from him,

but then we discovered a chink in the armor. An old friend of mine (well, pretty much an old enemy of mine) from California had found me and was threatening to blow our cover. His name was Jake, and he would be visiting his grandmother every summer in Odyssey. Because it was now wintertime, Jake was back in California. So, if he was able to communicate with my father, he might have told him where we were. Jake had been mad at me for years for turning him in for possession of a weapon. He'd had to go to a juvenile detention center, and I was sure he blamed me. I didn't doubt that he wouldn't think twice about putting my mom and me in danger, so my mother's news wasn't all that surprising.

"Mr. Henson called me today," she said. Mr. Henson was one of the agents who was assigned to keep us hidden. "Your father's been traveling. He hasn't moved anywhere, settled down in a house, or anything. He's just driving around the country, asking lots of questions."

"Does Mr. Henson think he's gotten any clues?"

"No, not yet. He's been going to all the obvious places. Like Louisiana." My mom was from Louisiana originally, and her family was still there. This probably meant Jake hadn't told him anything yet. "So, Mr. Henson doesn't think your dad has any leads."

"Did you tell Mr. Henson about Jake?"

"Yes," she said. "He knows about Jake. He can't tell if Jake is a threat or not. But he'll have someone keep an eye on him."

"What are we gonna do?"

"Just keep your eyes open. If you see your dad anywhere,

you call the police immediately. Here," she said, handing me a cell phone. "You take this wherever you go—to school, to Kidsboro—everywhere. The speed dial is set. If you see him, you just press this button, and you'll get Mr. Henson. Okay?"

I nodded and stared at the cell phone. My eyes watered, and Mom noticed.

"It's gonna be okay," she said and hugged me.

We knelt on the floor and prayed together, a defense we never had when we were in California. But now that we were Christians, we had a God who was bigger than any danger we might face. I was calmer when I stood up, and so was my mom.

• • •

On my way to Kidsboro, I wanted to stop by Whit's End to tell Mr. Whittaker about everything. He was the only person in Odyssey besides my mom and me who knew the truth about our situation. He had helped us through painful times before, and I wanted to talk to him now.

I walked up to the door of Whit's End, but couldn't bring myself to walk through it. I was still angry with him.

• • •

I made it to Kidsboro after lunch and immediately noticed a crowd on the shore of the creek. Nelson had created a game out of the Water Moccasin trips. Every team of two had 10 minutes to get as far as they could. At the 10-minute mark, Nelson blew his whistle, and the team had to retreat. So far, only one team, two boys with muscular legs, had made it beyond the borders of the tall fence upstream. Eventually, when the crowds waned, I imagined that Nelson would let somebody explore for a while and go as far as they wanted. But for now, with the crowds lined up, there had to be a limit.

Everyone was having a good time, except for the people and business owners of Bettertown. The bowling alley was empty. Scott was standing around with no pins to reset.

Max was talking to Rodney Rathbone, a school bully who had, for a short time, been a citizen of Kidsboro. Rodney was a pretty tough guy, and I wondered if Max was having him perform a little bouncer duty—though I couldn't imagine who he would be kicking out of what. There was no one in the whole town.

Suddenly, they both turned and walked purposefully toward the bridge. Nelson looked up and caught Max's gaze. Everyone must have wondered what Max was up to.

There was a noticeable smirk on Max's face as he crossed the bridge and stormed toward Nelson. He had a manila folder in his hand. A team had just parked so the vessel was halfway on the shore.

"Okay," Max said loudly. "Everybody off my property."

"What?" Nelson said.

"I own this land, and I want everyone off of it."

"This is Kidsboro, not Bettertown."

"I still own part of Kidsboro, and this deed proves it." Max pulled a contract out of his folder. I wove through the crowd to see what he was talking about. "As you can read here, I bought this land two months ago and built these houses on it." He pointed to four houses, the ones with cardboard siding, the "Creekview Estates."

I looked at the deed. My signature was on the bottom, along with the other four members of city council. We had, indeed, sold him the land.

"Take it," Max said, pointing to Rodney. Rodney grabbed the Moccasin and pulled it out of the water. He dragged it across the grass toward Nelson's house.

"You can't do this," Nelson said. "You don't even live here anymore."

"Sir, you need to hush up and get off my property," Max said, pointing a finger in Nelson's face.

This was the only place in Kidsboro where Nelson could launch his boat. There was a drop-off everywhere else. Max had successfully ruined the Moccasin business, and there was nothing we could do about it.

• • •

Later that afternoon, Nelson walked into my office without knocking. "He's imposing tariffs on all goods made in Kidsboro," he stated. Tariffs, in the real world, are taxes placed on things made in another country. For example, if you import something from France, you have to pay extra—a tariff. It encourages people to buy things from their own country, instead of a foreign country.

"If anyone from Bettertown buys something over here, they have to pay a tax on it before they can go back over the bridge. Max even stationed a guard there to make sure they're not smuggling anything in."

I walked out my door and saw a boy standing on the bridge, checking the jacket pockets of an innocent pedestrian just trying to get across the creek.

"This means," Nelson continued, as if I didn't understand what it meant, "that we'll be buying stuff over there, but they'll probably stop buying stuff over here because of the tax." I knew this affected Nelson more than anyone, because he sold his inventions every day.

• • •

The city council met within an hour to discuss our strategy for dealing with Max's scheme. He had already dismantled our best industry, and he had chiseled little holes in the rest of them. We had to do something, or Bettertown would overtake us.

Nelson had an idea. "Why is Kidsboro better than Bettertown?" This was a fair question, and it was a little disconcerting how long it took us to come up with an answer.

"We don't have Max," Jill said.

"Exactly. And what is Max doing over there?"

"He's putting everything under his control."

"Precisely. Bettertown is run by a power-hungry dictator, but in Kidsboro, there's freedom. We can do whatever we want. We have the freedom to make a life for ourselves. We can follow the American dream, get an education, create a business, and own a home," Nelson said proudly.

"What're you getting at?" Jill asked, having heard enough of the patriotic speech.

"Let's make those people realize that there's a better life

over here. That there's more to life than feeding and pampering tourists."

"How?"

"We offer them a chance to follow the American dream."

"Could you be a little more specific?" Jill said, glancing at her watch for effect.

"We go over to Bettertown and tell them what they're missing."

By the end of the meeting, Nelson had explained his strategy. Kidsboro would offer a "Starting Your Own Business" course. We had a fantastic teacher, Nelson, so we just needed students.

We headed out, just like a group of army recruiters. All we needed was a few good men.

• • •

We all watched as Nelson gave an incredible sales pitch to a boy named Jerry, the Bettertown garbageman. Then, trying to imitate the master we had just seen at work, we went out on our own.

The first person I ran into, unfortunately, was Scott. There was one person bowling, and Scott was setting up the pins for him. When he stood back up, he saw me and immediately looked the other way. I approached him.

I knew that the best way for me to open up to him would be to apologize. But I still thought he was making a big mistake, and I think my ego got in the way of my brain when I started off with the sarcastic remark, "Looks like you're having a blast."

"Why don't you go home?" he rolled his eyes.

"You're being stubborn."

"You still think you own me."

"I can understand you being mad at me, but how can you pick this place over Kidsboro?"

"Pardon me for taking up space, but I hope Kidsboro goes down the toilet. I really do. I think you guys need to be taken down a few notches."

"Why are you talking like that? This is not you. It's like . . . you've been brainwashed."

"Why? Because Max has told me that I can have a better life *here* than over there? Sounds familiar. Who's really doing the brainwashing, Ryan?"

I stared at him for a few seconds, and then put my head down and turned away.

• • •

Nelson and Jill had recruited one Bettertownian (or "Maxite" as many liked to call them) each to come to our seminar. I had struck out on my three tries. Max had penetrated their brains with too much propaganda, so there was no hope in getting them to come to the seminar. Alice bullied two kids into coming. I'm sure they were there for fear of their very lives.

Nelson and I, along with the four potential recruits, arrived in the meeting hall. Nelson would handle the presentation, and I would offer my two cents, though Nelson had much more experience than I did in starting a business.

Nelson was well prepared, in spite of having come up with this idea only the day before. He presented a strong case for owning your own business, as opposed to working for someone else. Then he offered some ideas for possible business ventures in Kidsboro. Two of the heads in the group nodded vigorously, as if they were seriously considering every word Nelson spoke. Jerry the garbageman looked especially interested.

Near the end of the meeting, when Jerry was practically ready to jump out of his chair and start building his new office, the door suddenly burst open. It was Max.

He looked at the Maxites. "What are you guys doing here?"

Jerry looked up innocently, apparently unaware that he was doing something wrong. "We were learning how to start our own business."

"Your own business?" Max asked in utter disbelief. "Did you ask permission to do this?"

"Permission?"

"Yes. You can't start your own business without my consent."

"What?" Jerry was offended.

"I might let you, but you *do* know that all your profits will be pumped right back into the government."

"You mean I can't keep any of my own profits?"

"Of course not. That's not the way our government works. You work for the city."

"But what if my business is in Kidsboro?"

"You can't live in Bettertown and work in Kidsboro."

"Why not?"

"Because it's against the law."

"What law?"

"Mine."

Jerry looked around at the rest of us, perhaps expecting us to defend him. But in the next moment, he seemed to muster the strength to do it himself. He faced Max. "Forget it! I'm not living my life to serve you!"

"You have no life without me!"

"What are you talking about?"

"In Bettertown, you have a nice house. You have a job. You're working for a team. When I found you, you were nothing," Max said.

"Yeah, and now I'm the garbageman."

"I can give you a promotion."

"To what? Bowling pin setter-upper?"

"You're violating the loyalty laws."

"I've got nothing to be loyal to. I'm moving to Kidsboro!"

"You move here, and you'll be broke before the spring thaw."

"I'd rather be broke than have to serve you."

Just then another voice of reason checked in. Harry, a Maxite, raised his hand. "Yeah, I'm moving to Kidsboro too." The other two Maxites lowered their heads, uncommitted to either side.

"You traitors!" Max yelled. "I'll get you back for this. Every one of you." I knew this message was directed at me as well as the others. Max stormed out and slammed the door.

• • •

That night as I was heading out of Kidsboro to go home, I noticed that Max and about 10 of his citizens were on the

Kidsboro side of the creek. He had floodlights illuminating the area, as if they were preparing for a long night. There was a pile of wood and wire to the side, and Max was ordering his subjects around. Scott was with them, looking cold, tired, and sick of working for Max.

What were they building?

• • •

I was in my real home eating breakfast the next morning when there was a knock at my door. Jill's face was pressed up against the screen door, and she was frantically knocking on the metal at the bottom.

Once I opened the door, she practically pulled my arm out of its socket. "Come on. You have to see this."

She dragged me through Kidsboro, toward the creek. Once we got there, my mouth fell open. I beheld a magnificent, yet horrifying, sight. Before me, on the edge of the creek, was a wall. Constructed out of wood and wire, it went around the circumference of the Creekview Estates. There were openings in the wall—well guarded by the wire—so I could see through it. Max and his merry band of Maxites were on the other side, taunting any Kidsborian they could see.

Max saw me and took the opportunity to anoint this structure as a tribute to himself. He turned to his flock, though I suspected the speech was really meant for me, and said, "This wall represents the hard work and dedication of a land that is driven by a desire to succeed. We constructed this wall because we will have nothing to do with failure, and we feel that the land on the other side of this wall represents the failure of government, and the failure of people. We are a separate, greater nation than Kidsboro! And from this moment forward, we will not allow Kidsborians on our land! They have infected us with the disease of greed and laziness. Now we will move on without them dragging us down to their level. We will rise as a new, independent nation—the nation of Bettertown!"

The crowd cheered with all the patriotism they could muster after a late night of building the monstrosity in front of them.

The wall was six feet high and about 30 feet long. On both ends there were perpendicular walls connected to it, which ran down to the creek side. All of it was well within the borders of the Creekview Estates. Max now controlled the bridge. There was an opening in the middle of the front wall, and I was sure that he would place a guard there at every moment of the day and would have a list of people who could and couldn't pass through it.

Of course, Kidsboro residents would be on the "no" list.

There was no good way to go *around* the wall. The drop-off down to the creek bed was fairly treacherous (except along the area where Nelson had sailed his Water Moccasin, which was also now controlled by Max). Plus, I was sure the guard that would be placed at the wall would also be in charge of keeping an eye on the bridge and anyone who tried to climb it from the underside.

In history class, we'd studied about how East and West Germany used to be separated by the Berlin Wall. For 28 years, those two countries were bitter toward one another, mainly because of their differences in opinion about government. I never understood why they would just cut themselves off from each other. I understood a little better now.

• • •

There was a lot of hurtful talk in Kidsboro the rest of the day: "We don't need them!" "Maxites are such idiots!" "I hate those guys!" "I'd like to knock that wall right on top of them!" Even people who were normally very rational, like Nelson, had their better judgment impaired by anger. Nelson spent the day inventing a catapult that would hurl things at the wall. Of course, Max had pulled the rug out from under Nelson's Water Moccasin, so quite possibly he had more to be angry about than most. But I didn't like how things were shaping up in our town.

SIX

BAD BLOOD

ON THE FIRST DAY of Christmas break, it all came to a head.

The first snow of the year had fallen on Odyssey, and about two inches covered the ground and rooftops. When I had left Kidsboro the night before, there was a guard at the wall. The same guard was there the next morning, as if he had stayed through the night. But I was pretty sure he was wearing different clothes.

My office door was blocked by a four-inch snowdrift, and I had to kick it out of the way to get inside. But as I was halfway through the door, I heard yelling. I turned and ran toward it.

Pete was standing on the Kidsboro side of the creek, about 20 feet downstream from the wall, and across the water was his friend Kirk. Kirk had been one of the Kidsboro defectors. He had joined Bettertown and seemed to be enjoying the change. But now it appeared that these two friends had become adversaries.

"What am I gonna do with this stuff?" Pete asked.

"I don't know. That's *your* problem," Kirk yelled back.

"What's going on?" I said as I approached Pete.

"I've got all this Bettertown money." He unfolded about 30 darbles. "And I can't use it anymore since I'm not allowed over there." He turned back to Kirk. "You have to exchange it for me," he yelled.

"We don't do that anymore. We don't give out tokens."

"Then I want real money!"

"Forget it!"

"Why not?"

"'Cause we don't have anything to do with you people anymore. We don't deal with your money; we don't deal with *you*."

"I spent good money for this, and you guys are gonna pay me back!"

"Make us!"

At this challenge, a number of Maxites gathered around Kirk, backing him up. Upon seeing the confrontation, several Kidsborians that were in the area filed in behind Pete.

"Come on over . . . or are you scared?" Kirk shouted.

"Why don't you come on over here, or won't your Mommy Max let you?"

Pete and Kirk stared at each other without blinking. Pete slowly bent down and grabbed a handful of snow. Kirk did the same. They packed it in their hands, making it more solid and easier to throw.

The rest of the group behind Kirk also reached down and filled their gloves with snow and purposefully began molding it together. Pete's group did the same.

Still, no one blinked.

Now it was five against five, each armed and dangerous, each one prepared for a battle but no one willing to throw the first snowball.

Deep down they must have all known, just like I did, that this would be the beginning of something bigger, something none of them could control. It would be war.

But for now . . . silence. No one dared move a muscle or even breathe suddenly. The rush of the creek was the only sound for 45 seconds.

The snowballs in their hands were as hard as they were going to get. Yet they continued to pack them, as if they knew that if the first hit didn't do its damage, all would be lost. The first hit was the crucial one.

Then it happened. A breeze blew in and shook the tree above the Maxites, blowing snow off one of its branches and sending it down Kirk's collar. Kirk scrambled to get it out. But Pete, who was concentrating on Kirk and not seeing the snow, interpreted the sudden movement as an act of aggression and panicked.

Pete threw his snowball, and it splattered on Kirk's left shin. Kirk seethed, and then the Maxites began machine-gunning their snowballs, pelting the group of Kidsborians. Kidsboro fought back, and I backed away from the fight, which was getting more and more intense.

Pete got smacked in the face and was stunned for a second, but then, with more determination than ever, he ran four steps closer to the creek and gunned his snowball into a Maxite stomach. His advance made him an easy target, and he was pummeled by three snowballs. He retreated.

The Maxites made use of their advantage and hid behind trees, coming out only to fire. Kidsboro was losing.

I had to stop it. I didn't know if anyone would listen to me, but Pete's face was as red as a cherry Popsicle, and the rest of the Kidsborians weren't looking much better. I ran out in the middle of fire.

"Stop!" I yelled. No one even heard me. The Maxites, sensing victory, had come out from behind their trees and were on the very edge of the creek. "Cease fire!" Still, no one listened. Suddenly, Mark, a Kidsborian, got smacked hard in the ear. He felt the side of his head for blood, and then he angrily charged the creek, eyeball-to-eyeball with the enemy. He was lambasted, one snowball hitting him so hard that it knocked him off balance. He lost his footing on the slippery snow and fell down, sliding over the four-foot embankment and into the creek!

He flailed around in the cold water, and Pete and I ran down to help him. The Maxites laughed but had enough sense to know that Mark could catch pneumonia, so they held their fire. Pete and I stepped down into the water and grabbed his arms. Mark found his footing on a rock and pushed himself up, and we pulled him onto the bank. He was soaked. His lips were already turning blue, and his entire body was shaking. Pete and I helped him toward home, and as we left, I looked back at the Maxites with a furious glare.

They smirked as if they had won.

• • •

This had gone too far. Surely Max had enough sense to realize that a war would not benefit anyone. As soon as I changed my pants and socks and returned to Kidsboro, I stormed directly to the wall. The guard stopped me.

"I'm sorry, but do you have any identification?"

"You know who I am, and I wanna get across."

"What was your name again?"

I rolled my eyes. "Ryan Cummings."

The guard picked up a clipboard with a list of names on it. He scanned it, and then shook his head. "I'm sorry. But you're not on the list."

"I'm talking to Max," I said, as I shoved past him.

He grabbed my arm fiercely and jumped in front of me. "First of all, you will address him as King Max. Second, you're not welcome in Bettertown. Now, turn around and go home."

"That's okay, Frank," Max said, crossing the bridge. "Let him pass. I'll talk with him."

"Yes, sir," the guard said, letting go of my arm and backing away. We headed to Max's clubhouse, or "palace" as the sign on the outside referred to it. We went into his enormous living area. It was almost as big as the meeting hall in Kidsboro. We sat down on cushioned chairs. I began to understand why people were drawn to living here.

"What's the problem?" Max asked.

"What's the problem? You didn't see the snowball fiasco this morning?"

"Oh, yeah, I caught the tail end of it. Shame about Mark. He shouldn't have charged the creek like that, very poor strategy."

"So, what are we gonna do about it?" I asked.

"Do?"

"Yes. We *have* to do something about this."

"Oh, I'm not sure that we do. I mean, I would hate to disrupt the natural order of things."

"What are you talking about?"

"People fight, that's a rule of life. This might be a good lesson for all of us."

"What kind of lesson—"

"Wasn't it you, Ryan," he interrupted, "who said that you liked the idea of having us around so that you could experience competition?"

"This is not competition. This is war."

"War is the greatest form of competition there is."

"Mark could've really gotten hurt, and he still might get sick."

"That's one of the hazards of war, Ryan. An excellent teaching point, don't you think?"

"No, I don't think! We have two towns here, and even though we have different philosophies of government, we don't have to fight about it. We could coexist. We could help each other; we could trade or barter. We could even combine our city councils and have common functions."

"Coexist? Oh, how boring. I'd much rather defeat you and take over the whole thing myself."

"Defeat us? What're you gonna do? Invade?"

"I could do anything I wanted to. You can't protect yourselves against me."

"What makes you so sure?"

"I've got more on my side than you think," he said with a wink. I had no idea what this meant, but it scared me.

"You've got nothing on your side but a bunch of robots who don't care anything about you or your town. They just like their balconies."

"And that's not worth fighting for?"

"They have no loyalty to you. My people? They're proud. They love their city. And they'll protect it with all they're worth."

"Well, your people may have pride, but we've got the strength." He smiled, and then pointed to the door. "It was nice talking to you," he said.

What did he mean he had the strength? Kidsboro had more people than Bettertown. And none of his population was especially athletic. Apparently, he had a plan.

• • •

On my way back into Kidsboro, I saw Pete and Nelson pounding a post into the ground at the site of the morning's snowball battle. I got a closer look and saw that the post had the day's date, then "The Battle of Snowy Creek," and Mark's name as the lone casualty.

"What is this?" I asked

"Something to help us remember," Pete said. "We might

need this for motivation later." It seemed that everyone on both sides of the creek was preparing for the inevitable.

• • •

Nelson was hyperventilating when he got to my office in the early afternoon.

"What's the matter?" I asked.

"I can't find my plans."

"What plans?"

He took a deep breath. "The catapult. You know that device I'm building to hurl things at the wall?"

"Right."

"Eugene and I drew a sketch before we started it. It had all the measurements, diagrams of every element. The sketch showed where everything would go. I even calculated angles, trajectory . . . Now it's all gone."

"Did you take it home with you?"

He shook his head. "It never left my clubhouse."

"You think somebody stole it."

He nodded.

• • •

I spent the rest of the day in my office, listening. I don't know what I was expecting to hear—another snowball fight, maybe an attack from the Maxites, or some sort of weapons testing from across the creek—but I was continually raising my eyebrows at any foreign sound. Being on edge like that was tiring. I usually stayed in Kidsboro until dinnertime, but on this day, I was worn out from worry. I headed home early.

When I went through my back door, I noticed that my mom had already decorated the Christmas tree. I had always helped her with that before, but with everything that was happening in Kidsboro, I hadn't had time. I felt bad, knowing that I had broken tradition. I'd barely even remembered that Christmas was coming up.

The phone rang. My mom wasn't anywhere to be seen.

"Mom?" I called. I heard the shower running upstairs, so I picked up the phone.

"Hello."

"Jim?" the voice on the other end of the line said.

It was my father.

"Jim, is that you?"

My instinct told me to hang up immediately. Talking to the man we had been hiding from for years was a dangerous thing to do. But for some reason, I stayed on the line.

"Jim, this is your dad. Don't hang up. I promise I'm not gonna hurt you."

"Why are you calling us?" I asked, a quiver in my voice.

"I just wanted to talk to you. My, you sound like a man. I miss you." He paused, as if he wanted me to return the sentiment. I didn't.

"Listen, I just wanted to tell you that I understand why you left. And . . . I don't know if you're gonna believe this or not, but I've changed. I'm not the man you knew when you were eight. And I don't expect your forgiveness, but I did want to let you know that I'm sorry."

The "I'm sorry" speech. I'd heard it many times as a child. He usually said those words as he surveyed the broken windows and lamps that he had destroyed the night before. I couldn't listen anymore. It hurt too much to hear those words again. It brought back too many bad memories. I hung up the phone.

My hand remained on the receiver, as though holding it down tightly would prevent him from calling back.

Mom came downstairs in a sweatshirt and jeans, drying her hair with a towel. "What's the matter? Are you calling somebody?"

I shook out of my trance and noticed my hand still on the phone. "It was Dad."

The towel dropped to the floor. Her mouth fell open; she was unable to speak for a full minute.

"What did he say to you?"

"He said he was sorry, and that he's changed."

"He knows where we are," she said under her breath.

"I guess I should've hung up."

"That's okay," she said. Her eyes darted around, then lit on me. "Why didn't you?"

"Hang up?"

"Yes."

"I don't know." This was true, though there was a voice inside that was telling me I enjoyed hearing his voice for some reason. Maybe I missed him.

My mom shook out of her own trance and got on the phone. She called Mr. Henson. He said he'd be right over.

• • •

Mr. Henson asked me more questions than I could answer. He peppered me with: "Did your father sound aggravated?" "Did it sound like long distance?" "Did you pick up any background sounds?" Seeing as how I was in total shock during the entire phone conversation, I couldn't imagine how he could think that I would pay attention to background sounds.

During this interrogation, my mom was sitting balled up on the couch, holding a pillow tightly to her chest. The phone rang, and everyone jumped. Mr. Henson ran to get on the extension upstairs and told my mom to answer it. As it turned out, it was just my mom's friend Margaret, wanting to know if Mom wanted to join her in a garage sale. Mr. Henson came back downstairs, quite agitated with Margaret.

Mr. Henson then called us together in the living room and gave us our options.

"You can move away if you want to," he said. "We'll protect you. We'll change your names again and move you somewhere in the Southeast, I think. Or you could stay here under our supervision, and if he comes back and provokes you in any way, we'll have him arrested on the spot. The fact that he knows your phone number doesn't mean he knows your whereabouts. We gave you a special number that gives callers no indication of your location. It's up to you."

Mr. Henson gave us a few more instructions on how to keep ourselves safe, and then headed for the door. He turned around momentarily. "It's a good sign that he called. If he were going to hurt you, he probably would've just shown up and done it. He knows that by calling, you have a chance to leave. So maybe he's being truthful. People do change sometimes."

We knew this was true. *We* had changed a lot over the course of the last few years. But my dad? I wasn't sure he was capable of it.

We stayed in a friend's basement that night. Still, I lay awake until three o'clock, worrying that the locked doors wouldn't be enough to stop a man motivated to hurt someone. I'm sure my mom stayed awake too.

SEVEN

BASIC TRAINING

ODDLY ENOUGH, THE NEXT morning I found solace in Kidsboro, even though we were on the brink of war. Maybe I felt that this was something I could control, or at least try to. In fact, I was in my office working on a proposal that would give me more control over the situation.

I was proposing an amendment to the city charter on how we would conduct war. Obviously, there was nothing in the original city charter about it, since there was no one around to have a war with when it was written. But an amendment was needed now. I would present this before the city council.

In the American government, the Congress has the responsibility to declare war. This is smart, making it a law that a lot of people have to agree on a decision as important as this one. So I figured it needed to be an overwhelming vote in the city council for Kidsboro to declare war. My proposal stated that 80 percent of the city council had to vote yes, which meant that four out of five of us had to vote in favor of war. Of course, with Scott being on the other side now, that meant it had to be unanimous. If the question were to come up right now, I would vote no. War could only end in disaster. But if we were forced to fight . . .

While I was scribbling away, the door opened and a person walked in with his or her jacket pulled over their head. I didn't think it was quite cold enough to be bundling up this much, so I immediately asked, "Who is it? What are you doing?"

The person took a quick peek outside to see if anyone was watching, then shut the door and lowered the coat. It was Marcy Watson, one of Jill's friends. Marcy had lived in Kidsboro almost from its beginning and had eventually become our banker. But she seemed to have grown bored with her job and was reeled in by Max's multimedia presentation. She was now a citizen of Bettertown and seemed to like it there. Jill was disappointed that she had moved away, but she understood Marcy's point of view. This was a mature way of handling it, of course, unlike my feelings toward Scott. Me? I had driven him away with my accusations that he was a traitor.

Marcy's eyes darted around the office until she found two tacks, and then she pounded her jacket into the wall, covering the window. This made it quite dark in my clubhouse. She definitely had my attention.

"What are you doing, Marcy?"

"I have to tell you something," she said.

"Okay."

"I'm sorry for abandoning Kidsboro, but that's over and done with now, and I have to deal with it. But I don't like what they're doing, so I have to tell you something."

"Okay."

"Because I don't want any of you guys to get hurt, I'm betraying my own city to lend you some important information."

"Okay."

"They're building an arsenal."

"Max?"

"Everyone. Max has got people working around the clock making snowballs. They've got a big pile four feet high. It's over by the school, blocked off by bed sheets so you can't see it. Plus, they have a weapon."

"Weapon?"

"A big catapult thing." The case of the missing catapult plans was solved. "It can heave big blocks of snow, about 10 pounds worth. It'll bury you."

"When do they plan on using it?"

"I don't know. Max has his own plans, and he's not telling anyone about them."

I swallowed a lump in my throat.

"I don't like what Max is doing, so I had to tell you this. Not that I think there's any way for you to stop him."

"Thanks," I said.

"I better get outta here," Marcy said, pulling her jacket off the window and draping it back over her head. She opened the door slowly and slithered out.

I had to call a city council meeting.

• • •

"We have to start an army," Alice said, pounding the table with her palm.

"She's right," Nelson said.

"We can't let these bozos push us around," Alice said. These two sentences equaled the most words she had ever spoken in a city council meeting. In war, she finally saw an opportunity to really inflict pain on someone without being accused of police brutality, which happened about every other week in Kidsboro.

I spoke up. "I don't want war."

"We have no choice," Jill said. "They're coming. You heard what Marcy said. Why would they be building up their arsenal if they weren't going to attack?"

"We have to prepare to defend ourselves," Nelson said. This made sense. There was no reason why we should just let them run over us.

"I don't want anybody to get hurt."

"That's what an army is for," Nelson said. "Listen, Ryan. An army is not there just to attack other people. An army is there to show other people that they can't attack *you*. At least, not without a fight."

I got up and paced around the room. The others were looking at me, silently pleading that this was the only solution.

"Okay, what do we do?" I asked.

"We recruit soldiers," Nelson said.

"We won't get enough people that way," Jill said. "If you haven't noticed, our city is made up of wimps. With the exception of Alice, we have a bunch of future figure skaters. They won't wanna fight. We need to have a draft."

A draft is when the government makes a law that every able man must serve in the army. It's only done during times of war.

"No," I said. "I don't want anyone in our army whose heart isn't in it. I'd feel guilty if something happened. We'll just have to depend on the patriotism of our people."

Jill didn't agree, but she nodded.

"Alice, I think you should be in charge of the army," I said. She straightened up and stood at attention. Nelson and Jill seconded this idea. "But," I pointed to Alice, "you will not train this army to attack. We're *not* going to be on the offensive here. You're only training them to defend themselves and their property." Alice's face turned down. For a split second she had probably envisioned storming the bridge. Her vision of greatness had just been erased.

"Nelson, I'd like you to build some kind of anti-missile device. We'll need to have something in case they use the catapult."

"Got it."

"Jill, you and I need to start recruiting."

"Okay."

"Let's go!"

• • •

Nelson advised us to get groups of people together and then start asking them to join our army, because no one would want to wimp out in front of his friends. This plan worked, and we recruited almost everyone in town. Jill and I also joined up and reported to boot camp just hours after we'd concocted this idea.

Alice, or "General Funderburk" as we were told to call her, was in top form that day. She lined us all up, and we stood at attention. She walked back and forth in front of us, inspecting whether or not we were standing up straight enough.

"You people are the sorriest looking soldiers I've ever seen," she said, shaking her head. She had seen dozens of army movies, and this was a scene that was in just about all of them. However, in this case it was probably true. I couldn't imagine a group of soldiers looking any sorrier. I peered down the line at our troops, and I didn't see much military promise.

There was Corey, the Kidsboro garbageman, who, when picking up the garbage, had to make twice the trips as most people because he had, as he put it, "a lifting problem."

There was James, the town doctor, who probably thought he was there to provide medical attention to injured troops. But we would all prefer to live with serious injury rather than let him treat us.

There was Roberto, who was born in the Dominican Republic and was not used to these cold temperatures. He was dressed in about eight layers of clothing, and this restricted his movement to the point where he really couldn't bend down to even form a snowball.

There was Pete, who held the record in our school for the most consecutive hours in front of a television—an amazing 23 hours. It was a weekend "Charlie Blue: Bird Lawyer" marathon.

There was Mark, who had no business being out after his traumatic creek accident but didn't want to be left out of the big war. His face was pale, and his lips were quivering.

There was Valerie, who didn't really want to be there, but

had developed a crush on one of the boys in Bettertown and wanted to impress him with her military experience. Of course, Valerie was more of a liability than an asset because she would distract our entire company, as practically every male in it had a crush on her. Also, if the temperature ever dipped below 20 degrees, she wouldn't risk possibly cracking her skin.

The others in line weren't much better. We weren't much of a fighting machine, but I was confident that Alice would get the best she could out of us.

• • •

Alice marched us to an area deeper in the woods, where Maxite spies couldn't watch us prepare. Then she had us run around with weights tied to our ankles.

"Come on, people! Move! This will prepare you for running through deep snow."

Then she had us crawl in groups of three. We had to fall to our knees in the snow, crawl a hundred feet to a tree, and then head back. My turn came, and I fell to the ground. A hundred feet suddenly looked like a mile. By the time I had neared the tree, my gloves were soaked through. My hands froze up on the turn. By the end of the course, I had to watch my hands carefully because I couldn't feel where I was putting them. I stood up and went back to the end of the line. I looked at Jill as if to say, "When are we ever going to need to crawl through the snow?"

By the time Pete had finished his round, his face was

caked with snow. He acted as if he didn't notice. The entire company had collapsed by the end of the exercise.

Next, we did snowball-throwing exercises. Alice had placed five targets on trees. Each soldier had to make snowballs, throw them, and hit all five targets in 25 seconds. Those who didn't make it would be pelted mercilessly by the rest of the company.

"Roberto! You're first!" Alice yelled. Roberto stepped forward reluctantly. The rest of us bent down and retrieved handfuls of snow. He watched us all very closely and cleared his throat.

So far, the exercises had been much harder for Roberto because of his eight layers of clothing. For him, crawling through the snow meant pretty much rolling through the snow. He dropped to his knees with a heavy plop and wiped the sweat off his forehead with the back of his soggy glove. He looked down at the snow and waited for the signal.

"Go!" Alice yelled. Roberto frantically grabbed a handful of snow and began packing it with his already numb hands. He packed it four times and created a loose ball. He turned, ready to throw his ammunition, but he got in too big a hurry. His follow-through was awkward because he couldn't lift his arm over his head, and he missed the target by four feet.

"Miss!" Alice shouted.

Time to panic.

He rolled over on his knees to make a new snowball and pounded it between his hands.

"The enemy's coming! Hurry up!" Alice yelled.

Roberto threw a desperation shot from his knees.

"Miss!"

No time to pack now. Roberto frantically clutched some snow in between his hands and threw it loose toward the target. The wind blew it back in his face.

"That's not gonna hurt anyone, come on!"

He lunged at the ground.

"They're coming at you with a catapult!"

He packed with reckless abandon.

"They're gonna bury you!"

He threw.

"Five seconds!"

Hit.

"They're on top of you!"

Too late.

"Time!" We all threw our snowballs, and Roberto was hit on every side of his body. Driven every direction by the force, he fell prostrate onto the ground. It grew quiet as we all looked down at Roberto, flat on his back as if he were about to make a snow angel. Alice shook her head and walked slowly toward him. She stood over him and stared down into his face.

"You're dead, soldier."

• • •

After we all took turns suffering the humiliation of that drill (Valerie was the only one who beat the timer), Alice took us over to our command post where we would make and store our arsenal of snowballs hidden behind two clubhouses and a bed sheet. Making snowballs and putting them in a pile was a welcome diversion from the workout we had just been put through, even though none of us could really feel our hands.

As I laboriously packed and stacked, Nelson came over to show me his plans.

"Here's my anti-missile device." He showed me a picture. It was a map of Kidsboro with something that looked like a net over it. "A mesh screen," he said. "We hang this in the trees over strategic targets—our houses, the base, and anything they catapult over here will be sifted into harmless flakes when it hits this."

"That looks good. How are we gonna get the mesh?"

"I'm working on it. Now, look at this." He showed me a rough sketch of some kind of launching device. "This is a salt shooter. I have bags of snow salt at my house. This device will send them—a few salt pellets at a time—into enemy territory and into their arsenal of snowballs. Now, it'll take a while, but after a couple of hours, the salt should have melted a good portion of the pile, or at least the snow will stick together and be worthless for throwing."

"How are you going to get it to be that accurate?"

"I'm working on that, too. I'll test it in my backyard before I bring it over. But listen, this way we can deplete their arsenal virtually undetected, since we're doing it just a few salt pellets at a time."

"That's brilliant," I said, holding the plans with both hands.

"Cummings!" Alice shouted at me. "Get back to work!" I guess she figured that she outranked me now that we were at war.

"You'd better show these plans to Alice," I told Nelson.

"All right."

• • •

After we had made a pile of snowballs about three feet high and seven feet wide, Alice marched us to the little league baseball field in McAlister Park and had us climb the backstop. She told us it was good training for climbing the wall between Kidsboro and Bettertown. I had no idea why we would need to do that, since I had told her that we weren't going to attack, but she seemed to think it was necessary.

This exercise was especially difficult because our hands were numb. But everyone managed to climb it anyway.

After that, we went back to the 25-second snowball drill, and this time, Roberto hit three of the targets before his time ran out. Eight people, instead of one, actually hit all five, and everyone came a little closer than they had before. Alice looked satisfied for the first time all day.

Alice dismissed us to our homes as the sun went down. Strangely enough, no one complained about the day, and no one hung his head low. Perhaps surviving the training exercises made us feel as if we had accomplished something.

Maybe we felt like we were ready.

• • •

The success of the day before may have been the reason I was a little too cocky for my own good the next morning. Max was reclined in my office chair when I walked in.

"Get any sleep last night?" he asked, smiling.

"Plenty." This was true. I had slept like a baby after the workout Alice had given me.

"Didn't stare at the ceiling last night, wondering when we're gonna strike and annihilate your little town?"

"Not at all."

"That's surprising, Ryan. You being so worried about your citizens like you always are. I figured you'd be a little more concerned about their well-being."

"I think you ought to be a little concerned yourself."

"Oh, really?" He sat up, ready to get down to business. "Do you enjoy war, Ryan?"

"Of course not," I replied.

"Of course not, no. You're a man of peace, aren't you? So, what would you say if I told you we could prevent this inevitable conflict between our two fair cities?"

"How?"

"I'll make you a deal. I'll call off my dogs, we sign a treaty, and the two of us live in peace and harmony."

"If?"

"If you give me back my wood."

I wasn't surprised by this request. Ever since I'd noticed that his "school" was made out of bed sheets instead of wood, I knew that Max was getting low on building material. Of course, across the creek, he saw our houses made of wood that used to be his. Naturally, he would ask for it back.

"Are you crazy?"

"It's *my* wood."

"We bought that wood from you."

"You don't need it now anyway. You've got your tarp and all that. Why don't you just use that?"

"That's not the point. You're talking about our houses. They belong to us."

"But isn't it a small price to pay for peace?"

I stiffened. "You're not taking our wood."

He stood up and smiled again. He acted as if he had come as an instrument of peace and had been thwarted by a warmongering dictator. He shook his head and said, "Then I'm sorry to say this, but . . . I'm afraid we're at war." He slapped me gently on the shoulder, and then turned and left.

EIGHT

THE RESCUE SQUAD

About three more inches of snow had fallen during the night, so our arsenal had to be dug out a bit. The footprints from the day before were gone. Evidence of our training had been buried.

Alice put us through more drills. We all ached from the day before, but none of us cared. We all seemed a little sharper, a little more determined, a little more excited about being there. Every person—except James the doctor—hit all five targets before time ran out. We were suddenly a well-oiled machine, a team of trained soldiers taught to protect each other with every freezing, pained bone in our bodies.

Halfway through target practice, I heard a *psst!* I was apparently the only one who had heard it. I looked around, but didn't see anyone. Thinking I had imagined it, I went back to the drill. Then I heard it again: "*Psst*!" I turned again and saw a small bit of a black jacket sticking out from behind a tree. I glanced around to see if anyone noticed me, and then I went to investigate.

It was Marcy.

"What's wrong?" I asked.

"You gotta call this off," she said, her eyes darting all around her.

"Call what off?"

"The war. Just give Max whatever he wants and forget it."

"Why?"

"He's brought in ringers."

"What?"

"He went around town yesterday and recruited a bunch of hoodlums—Rodney Rathbone, Luke Antonelli, Jerry Wilmott, and lots of others." Jerry and Luke were pitchers on the Odyssey Middle School baseball team. Rodney wasn't the athletic type, but he could probably give the Bettertown army some tips on cheating.

"What do those guys have to do with this? Why did they even want to be involved?"

"Are you kidding? This is a war. There might be an opportunity to pound someone. You think they'd pass that up?"

"I guess not." I looked at the troops, loyally preparing to defend their city, and I knew in my heart that we didn't have a chance against those guys. At least, not if we pitted strength against strength.

"Would you do me a favor, Marcy?"

"Sure. Anything."

"Keep an eye on 'em. Let me know if they're planning an attack."

"Okay."

"Thanks."

Marcy hurried off for fear of being discovered. I rejoined my unit.

We still had one advantage over them. With Nelson on our side, we were smarter. If we could out-strategize them, we had a chance. I casually went over to Nelson, who was watching the drill.

"How much longer before that salt shooter is up and running?"

"It's ready."

• • •

We set it up under the tree that was closest to the creek, where we could still escape detection. The salt shooter looked like a narrow-barreled cannon. Nelson poured an entire 10-pound bag of salt in the back of it, and then motioned for me to climb the tree. I took a pair of binoculars with me to scout out the guards around the snowball pile while we shot the salt at it.

I started up the tree. Nelson checked the wind, and there was none. I continued to climb until I could just see the guards' heads over the sheets, shielding the snowball pile. The pile was higher than they were. I nodded to Nelson, and he turned the machine on. It revved up for a couple of seconds, and then it made a *phht!* sound, like an air pump. A dozen or so pellets flew out, and I quickly put the binoculars to my eyes to see where they landed. The sheet puckered all over.

"You hit the sheet. Aim it farther," I said. "You'd better go real far so you don't hit the guards."

"Gotcha," Nelson said, adjusting the machine. The cannon

rose up a bit, and he was ready again. Another dozen pellets flew out with a *phht*! I looked through the binoculars and saw the pellets hit the snow behind the pile.

"About 10 feet back this way."

Two adjustments later and Nelson had it. I saw the pellets hit the snowball pile. The guard in front looked up as if he'd heard the sound of rain. The sky was perfectly clear, so his eyebrows rose a bit. Then he seemed to brush it off. Nelson shot another round. Bulls-eye. The guard looked around again, thoroughly confused. I chuckled at this funny sight.

Nelson hit the target fairly consistently with the next five shots, and every time the guard looked around, he saw nothing and probably thought he was going crazy. He went over to talk to someone else and . . .

Suddenly I saw something through the binoculars that I wasn't expecting. In front of the sheet were several guards pulling someone forcefully toward Max's office. The person they were pulling was struggling to get away, like a dog being taken to the vet. The struggle continued until the victim came out of the jacket and fell to the ground. It was a black jacket.

Marcy.

They'd captured our spy.

I hurried down out of the tree and gave the binoculars to Nelson.

"What's wrong?"

I didn't answer. I went straight to Alice.

• • •

"We have to form a rescue team," Alice said without hesitation.

"How are we gonna rescue her? We can't even get through the wall." This was barely even a question to Alice. The wall, the bridge, and the creek were not obstacles to her.

The bridge was the only legitimate way to get across the creek. The water was from three to six feet deep. During the summer, it was possible to wade through it, but the cold was a factor now. Upstream from the bridge, the drop-off was too extreme. It was like falling off a cliff. Downstream from the creek, there was the threat of getting caught in the current and going over the waterfall. This was the reason that control of the bridge was so crucial to this war. There was no other way across.

"We'll get across," Alice said. I thought that maybe she was thinking of taking out the guard at the wall, but now that Max had recruited the thugs of the school, he had a guy even bigger than Alice there, plus another one on the other side of the bridge.

"How?" I asked.

"We'll get across," she repeated. We went to the troops.

"Men," Alice said to the unit, "I have a dangerous mission that we must undertake. One of our brave soldiers has been captured by the enemy." Everyone started looking around, trying to see who was missing. "We have to form a rescue team, go into hostile territory, and bring her back."

"*Her?*" Pete asked. "Who?"

"Marcy," Alice said.

"Marcy's a Maxite."

"She was spying for us. Now she's been found out. No telling what kind of torture they're putting her through over there. We have to go. I need two good men."

The problem of getting over the creek probably never even crossed anyone's mind. The thought of wandering behind enemy lines did. There were no immediate volunteers.

"I think I should go," I said. I felt responsible, since I was the one who had asked her to be our spy. She might have been trying to get information for me when she was captured.

"Good," Alice said. "We need one more."

Jill stepped forward. "Marcy's my friend. I'll go."

"All right. We have our team. Come on." Alice motioned for us to follow her. The rest of the unit went back to their stations.

• • •

Alice took us back to her real house. We followed her into the garage, where she pulled out a toboggan. She also pulled out two large pieces of wood and a long rope, and then handed them to us. I saw Jill's eyes widen, as if she were wondering, as I was, what in the world we were going to do with this stuff.

"Put these on," she said, handing us white parkas. "It'll camouflage us against the snow." She also made us put white stuff that looked like cold cream on our faces.

Without a word, she led us back into the woods, to a point well east of Kidsboro. We were far downstream of the bridge, past the waterfall, nearing the farm owned by Tom Riley, a friend of Mr. Whittaker's. As Alice stopped, I had an inkling of what she had in mind—and it terrified me.

At this point in the creek, there was a steep hill that led to the creek bed. The cliff on the other side of the creek was five feet lower than on this side.

She wanted us to jump it.

She went down to the cliff edge and set up a ramp with the two pieces of wood we had brought. Jill and I stayed back and contemplated our certain death.

"Is she crazy?" Jill asked.

"I think so," I said. It was a seven-foot drop into freezing water if we didn't make it.

Alice covered the ramp with snow and then tied the long rope to a tree. She threw the other end of the rope across the creek. It landed on the other side. I presumed this was how we would get back across once we had made the daring rescue.

She headed back up the hill. She wouldn't look either of us in the eye.

"Have you ever done this before?" I asked.

"No," Alice said, apparently finding no relevance to this question. "Lean forward as we're going over. And wrap your legs around the waist of the person in front of you." She casually hopped into the toboggan and held the reins. Jill and I exchanged looks.

"What's wrong?" Alice asked.

I had no feeling in my legs, but somehow I managed to climb in behind Jill. I grabbed tightly to the ropes along the side of the toboggan and stared down at our doom. I turned away quickly. Jill was shaking in front of me. Alice was a rock.

"Push off," she said, and we did, as hard as we could, believing speed was our friend.

We picked up speed . . . faster . . . faster . . . the creek came on like an oncoming train. The cold wind tore at my face. I couldn't watch, but I couldn't *not* watch.

I looked ahead and suddenly realized that we had veered too far right. We were going to miss the ramp!

Alice leaned to her left, and we went with her. Jill lifted her head, realized what was happening, and screamed. We weren't going left.

The cliff was 40 feet away . . . 30 . . . 20 . . . 15 . . .

"Bail!" Alice screamed and dropped off the left side, taking us with her. The impact drove my face into the snow, and I went into an uncontrolled roll. Jill flipped over onto her head, kicking me in the face. Before I stopped, I saw Alice lunge for the toboggan, grab one of the side ropes, and save it before it plummeted off the cliff.

Jill was face down.

"You okay?" I asked. She lifted her head long enough to say "yes," and then buried it again. I felt a lump forming on the side of my head.

Alice was already up and ready to do it again. She said, "My fault. I misread the terrain."

Jill rolled over and looked straight up into the sky. "She's not going back up the hill, is she? Please tell me she's not going back up the hill."

"She's going back up the hill."

Alice gave us a few moments to catch our breath, and then she yelled down to us from the top of the hill. "Come on, let's go!" We both shook our heads and trudged back up.

I was a little firmer with her this time. "Are you *sure* this is gonna work?"

"Yeah," she said, grabbing the reins. Jill and I took our places on the sled. Without any hesitation, Alice pushed off, and we joined her.

The toboggan gained speed . . . faster . . . The ramp approached, only this time we were straight on. We were going to do it.

I prepared to lean forward, the snow kicking in my face. I clenched my teeth, peeked at the ramp, and suddenly . . .

Woosh! We were airborne! The toboggan tipped up ever so slightly, but then lost speed at the zenith and plummeted back down. The front of the toboggan dipped at a severe angle. I squeezed the side ropes with all my might. The sled swooped down and . . . *Wham!* The curled wood at the front slammed into the bank. The back flipped over the top of us, sending us headlong into the snow. The jarring knocked the wind out of me.

My face was pinched between the ground and the topside of the toboggan. Jill was pretzeled up beneath me. Alice detached herself from the side ropes and quickly stood up.

We'd made it.

"Are you okay?" I asked Jill. She lifted the ski cap off her face and looked at me. She chuckled.

"I'm fine."

I started laughing too. Soon we were in hysterics, simply happy to be alive.

Alice was on to business, of course. By the time Jill and I

had stopped laughing, Alice had tied the loose end of the rope to another tree. She pulled it taut and hung underneath it to make sure it would hold us when we came back and needed to get across. She was satisfied and was ready to rescue somebody.

She led us the long way around Bettertown. She felt it would be best to move in from the back.

As we got close enough to see the clubhouses of Bettertown, Alice motioned for us to get down. The closer we got, the slower we moved and the more we relied on trees to shield us. "Okay, I'm going to that tree. Jill, you follow along, exactly one tree behind me. Ryan, you're one tree behind her."

"Got it," we said at the same time.

Alice moved with quick, smooth steps to the next tree, then the next. I watched Jill do the same, and I followed along behind as I'd been told to do. Soon, I could hear voices. Luke Antonelli was giving orders to a smaller kid who I didn't recognize from this distance.

Then I saw it: their arsenal. A huge pyramid of snowballs, standing six feet tall and as wide as a minivan. It was more ammunition than they would need for a dozen wars.

Then I saw something even more frightening—the weapon. They'd obviously taken Nelson's plans and expanded on them, like doubling the recipe for a cake. The catapult looked exactly like Nelson's, only it was three times bigger. The springs that would fling the snow were made out of iron coils as thick as watermelons. Nelson had intended to use a mop bucket to hold the ammunition on his catapult. On this one, it was an outdoor garbage can.

They could probably bomb Indiana with it.

I listened carefully, trying to hear what the enemy was saying while still trying to keep up with Jill and Alice. I could make out some of the conversation. Max was talking with Rodney Rathbone.

"What do you want me to do with her?" Rodney asked him. I assumed they were talking about Marcy.

"Move her into the rec center. I'm tired of listening to her whine." I could tell that Alice heard the conversation as well, because she changed directions and headed toward the rec center.

I was 10 feet away from the snowball mountain and could clearly see the checkered pattern on the guard's ski hat. Alice moved along, undetected, and Jill followed.

Then something strange happened. I felt something hit me . . . like tiny grains of hail. A few seconds later, I was hit by another batch. This time, I could hear them falling all around me. The guard turned to see what had made the noise.

It was the salt pellets!

I quickly ducked back behind my tree, held my breath, and hoped the guard hadn't caught a glimpse of me. The pellets again rained against the tree I was hiding behind. I heard the guard shuffle around and move closer. The footsteps got louder. More pellets. The wind must have changed and carried the pellets farther than Nelson was aiming. The guard, curious about this strange noise, continued coming. I pressed myself as flat as I could against the tree, wishing I could climb inside of it.

I turned my head . . . and he was there. His face was inches from mine, his nostrils flaring.

"Rodney!" he shouted. I tried to run, but it was too late. The guy grabbed me and forced my arm behind my back. Rodney ran up, discovered Jill, and went after her, too. A couple of other guards went for Alice, who fled the scene and headed back from where we had come.

Jill and I were taken with rough hands to the rec center, where Marcy sat quietly. Her hands were tied behind her back, and Rodney ordered the same to be done to us. Neither Jill nor I struggled. We knew we were outnumbered.

I looked at Marcy, who didn't seem to have been tortured, but I asked anyway. "Are you all right?"

"Yeah."

"I'm sorry."

"That's okay."

A couple of Maxite thugs tied our hands behind our backs and around the wooden supports that helped hold up the roof. Marcy's hands were wrapped around another one. The three of us sat on the ground.

"Have they been bad to you?" I asked her.

"Every 10 minutes they come in and put snow down my back. I'm starting to get used to it."

The icy ground was beginning to penetrate my pants and numb up my legs. I could tell the same thing was happening to Jill because she shifted a few times and then settled on a bent knee approach to sitting. Apparently Marcy's legs were already numb because she sat still.

Over the next few minutes, I had fleeting thoughts of trying to escape, but I knew it was probably not possible. Even if I did manage to free all of us without anyone noticing, we would still have to get past several guards, all of whom outweighed me by about 20 or 30 pounds. So I sat quietly, being the model prisoner.

Suddenly Marcy said with glee, "Hey, this is just like your dream, Jill. The one where you and Ryan get stuck in a room together all alone." Jill's eyes widened.

"Marcy—" she said through clenched teeth, trying to sound both serious for Marcy's sake and indifferent for my sake.

Marcy went on, ignoring Jill's objections. "Of course, *I* wasn't there. And in your dream, didn't Ryan put his arm around you and try to comfort you? Guess he can't do that now, with his hands tied . . ."

Jill's face turned hot pink. She turned and gave me a nervous smile. "Marcy, nobody cares," she said, again trying to sound indifferent.

She dreams about me?

Much to Jill's obvious relief, the tension broke when the door opened and Kirk walked in. He stopped suddenly, as if he wasn't aware that I would be in there. He looked at me. Kirk was a former Kidsborian. I was the one who had put him up for a vote in the city council, and now he was my enemy.

He had a handful of snow. He had probably been ordered

to put it down our backs. He looked only at me. But not as an enemy. He was looking at me as the one who gave him his start in Kidsboro.

He crushed the snow in his fist and dropped it on the ground. Then he turned around and went out the door.

• • •

An hour passed, and the three of us had said very little to each other. Jill could barely even look at me after Marcy's embarrassing revelation. Activity outside the door seemed to be growing, and I wondered if an attack was imminent. My town was on the brink of being shelled, and here I was, stuck in this room, unable to help. My frustration was growing.

The door burst open, and Max came in. He chuckled upon seeing us, helpless, our rear ends frozen to the ground. Then he approached me.

"Feeling beaten, Ryan?" I didn't respond. "Well, you are." He crouched down and looked me in the face. "That was a nice little rescue attempt. I commend you. Very brave, too. But I hope you noticed something about your attempt. It was a failure. Just like everything you've done lately. And yet, everything I've laid my hands on has turned to gold. Did you see that arsenal I've got? Have you looked at the size of my guards? How about that catapult? We're stronger than you. We're better, faster, and smarter. And if you know what's good for you, you'll stop this little war we've got going before it even starts."

"We're not giving back the wood," I said with a stiff upper lip, which wasn't difficult since it was frozen.

"Ryan!" Max laughed. "I'm surprised at you. You're going to willingly put your town through a devastating war, when you could just swallow your pride and get it over with now."

I stared at the ground in front of me. Was I being prideful?

Max moved even closer to my face and got serious. "You've got until Monday to give me back my wood. At three o'clock on Monday afternoon, we attack and take the wood by force." He stood up and headed out the door. I swallowed a lump in my throat and exhaled. I turned to Jill, who seemed to empathize with my dilemma.

Crash!

Suddenly the wall caved in, almost landing on the three of us. Jill and Marcy screamed. The ground shook under us. Alice cracked her knuckles and stepped over the wall that she had just pushed in.

I could hear the Maxite army come to life as Alice jerked the support beams out of the ground with ease and freed us. Rodney and some others burst through the door, looked a little stunned as they saw the room had one less wall, and then came after us.

In true Hollywood fashion, Alice smiled at Rodney and said, "Sorry to bust in on your little party."

We ran. Jill and I led the way, with Marcy right behind us and Alice falling back on purpose to deter anyone from chasing us.

It was difficult to run with our hands still tied behind our backs, but on we sped, toward the rope that was hopefully still tied across the creek. I looked back and saw that there were six Maxites behind us, but none of them seemed to be running their hardest for fear they would actually catch up to Alice.

By the time we reached the creek, we had lost them. The rope was still there. Alice untied us, and we made it back across. Out of breath, Marcy thanked us. It was sort of a weird rescue, but a rescue nonetheless.

NINE

WAR

WHEN MR. WHITTAKER FOUNDED Kidsboro, he told us that he would be available to answer questions and give advice. I rarely asked for advice because I wanted to figure things out on my own. But this was a problem I didn't know how to handle. Still, I wasn't sure I could trust him anymore. I didn't know whose side he would be on in a war. So I missed my weekly meeting with him again.

I did know that going to war against Bettertown should not be my decision alone. Technically, it was a decision for the city council, but I thought this was too important to bring before only four citizens out of 25. I had to bring this up before the entire town. It was their houses and their town that were at stake.

We held an emergency meeting in the pavilion. Everyone was there. When I walked in, I noticed that there wasn't the usual hubbub that a group of 25 adolescents and preadolescents makes. People spoke in low tones with furrowed brows. Others shook their heads in disbelief at what was happening.

I took my place in front. I didn't have to call them to order. They were already staring up at me like little children waiting for their parents to make the bad dreams go away. I wished I could.

I breathed a long sigh and began. "We have a decision to make, and I think everyone in town should be here to help make it. Max has threatened to attack and rip apart our houses if we don't agree to give him back his wood by three o'clock Monday. I've been over there and seen their arsenal. This is the situation: They have a snowball pile twice as big as ours. They have recruited some of the toughest guys in our school to be in their army—including Luke Antonelli, Rodney Rathbone, and Jerry Wilmott." I saw a few people exchange concerned looks when I mentioned those names.

"I know that it would be a pain to take apart our houses, but we do have tarp now, and I think we could get by with that. It's just something to think about." I stopped to get input from them, but they didn't take the hint. They just sat there, as if they were expecting me to list our assets alongside the large list of liabilities I had just rattled off. Actually, I didn't see too many assets. "I'd like your input," I told them.

"Let 'em come," came a voice from the back. It was Alice. "We're ready." A few people clapped in agreement.

"We'll never win, no matter how ready we are," said Valerie, an unwelcome voice of reason. "We can rebuild the town. Let's just give him the wood, get rid of all memories of Max, and move on with our lives."

"But we can't get rid of him," Nelson said. I was surprised that he would contradict his sister. "We all know Max. We know he'll never quit wanting more. If we give him the wood, what is he going to want next? Will he try to expand his kingdom and take the land to the east and west of us? How many more businesses can he run into the ground just because he's there and he hates us? We can't get rid of him. I say we fight him."

"I agree," said Mark. "We can't just let Max and his friends run over us whenever they want to."

"And Nelson's right," Marcy said. "They *will* want to. Every chance they get, they'll try to invade, especially if they know they can just plow over us."

People were nodding their heads furiously, and I tried to restore reason. "Do you understand what you're saying? You actually want to stay here and try to protect our houses while Max and his troops come over here and attack? I'm sorry to say this, but . . . they're *stronger* than we are. Some of those guys are athletes—they're huge! I'm not sure we stand a chance."

"You're wrong," Jill said. She walked up to me, and I took a step backward. "We've got one thing those guys don't have. We've got pride. We've got loyal citizens. We've got a country worth fighting for."

The crowd cheered, ignoring the fact that we weren't a country.

"Our army has been working hard, not because we have to, but because we love our freedom. Nelson knows what he's talking about. If we give the Maxites this victory, we'll never be free from Max's rule. We might as well crown him king. Are you people ready to make Max king of Kidsboro?" Jill asked loudly.

"No!" the crowd unanimously declared.

"Then we have to fight."

"Yes!"

Everyone looked up at me. I was glad that it had been taken out of my hands. It had become their decision. "Okay. On Monday, we go to war."

The troops cried out in agreement, many standing to applaud. There was no more tension, no more fear. Kidsboro would not be Bettertown's doormat anymore. We would fight.

• • •

The crowd filed out of the building and headed for the creek, half wanting to tell the Maxites about our decision and half wanting to attack right away. There were eight Maxites on the other side of the creek, downstream of the wall, and several Kidsborians mirroring them on our side. The Kidsborians taunted them. The Maxites bent down and made snowballs just in case. Our people did the same. Names were thrown over from both sides—hatred at its worst.

Then I saw Scott. He was behind the line of eight, and he made a snowball and joined in the name-calling. The yelling became so fierce that no one could even decipher any of the words. There was just a lot of pointing and clenched fists. Scott looked at me, his teeth clenched. We stared at each other for a few moments, and my only thought was that I couldn't wait to deck him with a snowball. I imagine he was thinking the very same thing.

• • •

I thought it was curious that Max made his threat on a Friday, and then gave us the weekend to think about it. But I figured it had less to do with him respecting the Sabbath and more to do with people on his side leaving town for the weekend. Whatever the reason, we had the next two days to think about things.

One thing I did during the weekend was go to the Kidsboro Community Church. It was made up of a group of wooden benches along the creek, upstream from the wall. Very few people ever attended, but I had gotten some good things out of it before, especially when I had decisions to make.

Joey, the preacher, was one of the two African-American citizens in Kidsboro. He was also the son of a real minister, and, though he didn't have quite the speaking gifts of his father, he poured out his heart and soul every week. I admired that.

Joey smiled at me as I approached. Once again, I was the only one present. In the front, next to the music stand he used for a pulpit, was a nativity scene. It had all the characters—Mary, Joseph, shepherds, wise men, angels, donkeys, and the baby Jesus lying in a manger.

I had seen nativity scenes before—we had one ourselves—but for some reason, this one looked different. More beautiful somehow. I couldn't quite put my finger on it at first, but then I realized that this was the first time during this Christmas season that I had even thought about the birth of Jesus. I glanced down at my watch. Today was December 22. Christmas had come and was almost gone, and I hadn't even paid attention.

None of the characters were talking—the shepherds, the wise men, none of them. Nobody was saying, "Boy, that was some trip," or "I hope you like this myrrh," or "Move your head! I can't see the baby!" This was the first time I had ever noticed that the only thing they were doing was staring at the baby Jesus. All those people, yet there was such peace on that night.

I sat down on the hard wooden bench, and Joey took out a hymnal. We sang three verses of "Silent Night." Neither one of us had much in the way of a singing voice, so we could barely be heard above the rush of the creek.

After the hymn, Joey made a couple of announcements. There was going to be a church-wide prayer vigil early Monday morning to pray about the war, and then a potluck dinner after the war was over. He put me down on the list to bring a vegetable dish and napkins.

He prayed, calling the war "an atrocity" and "needless," and asking God to intervene and make sure that no one got hurt. I repeated his "Amen."

Joey handed me the offering plate, and I saw him look up at something behind me. I turned around to look.

It was Scott.

He came up quietly, sneering my way a little, and sat down on the farthest possible seat from me. I stood up and carried the offering plate to him. He took it without making eye contact, and I returned to my seat. Joey seemed a little disappointed that neither of us gave anything, and when he was ready to speak, he looked at both of us with disdain, as if he had the perfect sermon with which to nail us.

He was right.

He read from Matthew 9 about how Jesus, the Savior of the world and King of Kings, didn't hang out with other kings and princes and military heroes. "His friends were fishermen," Joey began. "And he spent time with tax collectors and sinners—people that were hated back then. The religious leaders asked his disciples, 'Why does your teacher eat with tax collectors and sinners?' Jesus loved these people and wanted to be their friends and help them change their lives.

"You see, Jesus didn't think of any group of people as his enemies. He didn't say, 'That guy hangs out with this group or that group, so I hate him.' He treated people as individuals." Joey cleared his throat and raised his voice, "How many times at school do we put people in groups? Oh, those are the jocks, or the bullies, or the stuck-up princesses, or the geeks . . . and so I don't like them. They're not jocks, or bullies, or princesses, or geeks. They're people. People who have feelings."

He glanced at both of us. "And now friends have turned into enemies, simply because they live in different places? What's up with that?

"Jesus told us to love our enemies because they're people, just like us. And if we give them a chance, they might even be our friends. You guys are making a mockery of the Christmas season. Jesus came as the Prince of Peace. The least you can do is give it a try yourselves."

Joey put down his Bible and waited for us to respond. I imagine he wanted us to kiss and make up, but we didn't. I don't know why. That was my best friend sitting over there, as far away as he could get from me. I'd slept over at his house dozens of times. We'd had dreams of one day being college roommates. I'd seen him in his Spiderman pajamas. He was my best friend, and I had placed him in a group because of where he lived, just like Joey said, and now I was supposed to hate him.

But I didn't.

Perhaps Kirk was a better man than I was, dropping the snow that was meant to go down my shirt. At least he knew that the value of friendship was more important than victory over an enemy.

Joey gave up and prayed a benediction. We stood up. Scott and I looked at each other, this time without hatred, and then he turned and walked away.

• • •

I got up Monday morning, and the first thing I heard outside the house was the sound of dripping. I stepped outside. The icicles were melting, and the temperature was getting warmer. I smiled, thinking this might mean a postponement of the war. We couldn't throw snowballs if there was no snow.

But my mother told me it was supposed to get colder in the afternoon and snow some more. I chose to believe the icicles.

Kidsboro was in full motion when I got there. Alice was in the meeting hall (now army headquarters), giving a briefing on the military strategy for the day. She'd put up an easel with a well-drawn map of Kidsboro and Bettertown on it. There were arrows and X's and little silhouettes of bombs on it. I certainly hoped she didn't really have any bombs for this battle.

I should have stayed to hear the strategy since I was in the army, but at the moment, I was clamoring and praying for another way out of this. I went to the creek side where I saw six people lined up on either side of the creek, just staring at each other. Every now and then, an insult was hurled, but for now, no snowballs. I went to the wall and tried to get past. The guard stopped me.

"What do you want?"

"I wanna talk to Max."

"About what?"

"Ending this war."

"You're giving him his wood?"

"No, I just want to—"

"I was told not to let you through unless you are offering to give him his wood."

"Let me talk to him."

"Sorry."

I took a sharp move to his right, trying to shove past him, but he stopped me and turned me around. I walked back to Kidsboro.

• • •

As it turned out, my mother was right. By one o'clock, it was starting to get colder, and it was snowing again. Ominous clouds gathered overhead.

I sat in on another of Alice's strategy sessions. She had a

plan to storm Bettertown's arsenal and destroy their pile of snowballs. I still didn't like the idea of being the attacker, but this wasn't exactly attacking *them*, so I didn't object.

Afterward, I went outside and saw several people taking last minute target practice. Nelson was up in a tree, spying on the Maxites with his binoculars.

"What are they doing?" I called up.

"They're moving the catapult closer to the creek, and they're transporting some of their snowballs with it. Plus, the troops are getting fitted with their gear—special backpacks that they're filling with snowballs."

Nelson came down and started putting his mesh up over the clubhouses. I helped him. He had stopped shooting the salt, seeing that it hadn't had much of an impact. It would be impossible to control the shots anyway, with the wind swirling around as fiercely as it was right now.

All this busy work was being done, but at this point, it was really just a waiting game.

• • •

At 2:45, the troops were already crouched down into position, with a pile of snowballs at each foot. Alice had people stationed in every area of town. The whole place was surrounded, most heavily around our arsenal. Even though each person in the army had his or her own set of snowballs, the big pile was hardly even dented. Running out of ammunition would not be likely.

The weather, however, might be a problem. The wind was kicking up and sleet was blowing horizontally into our faces. Because of the thick clouds flying overhead, it was dark—almost like dusk—even though it was the middle of the afternoon.

I knelt in position, with my pile of snowballs nearby, and peered around at the tense faces.

Jill wiped her face with her sleeve quickly, so as not to block her eyesight for more than a split second, in case they decided to attack early.

Nelson was our lookout man in the trees, his eyes buried in the binoculars. I could see him shivering because of the wind. The tree he was in swayed dangerously back and forth, but he didn't seem to notice.

Mark was making more snowballs, thoughtlessly increasing his pile. Just to make sure.

Alice stood closest to the creek, staring the enemy in the face, daring them to come. She had no ammunition.

I could barely see the Maxites across the creek because of the darkness and snow, but I could tell they were preparing to come across. They were getting into a double-file line.

The wind howled around us. Other than that . . . silence.

Ring!

What was that? It was coming from my jacket. My cell phone was ringing—the one my mother had given to me so I could call for help if I saw my father. But it had never rung before. I reached into my pocket and pulled it out. I pushed the talk button.

"Hello?"

It was my mom. The connection was bad. I could barely make out "Ryan, get home now—" *Click.* What had happened?

Had the phones gone out? It was probably the weather. But maybe not.

Maybe somebody had grabbed the phone out of her hand.

Maybe my father had hung up the phone.

"I gotta go." I stood up and ran as fast as my numb legs could carry me.

The troops couldn't believe I was chickening out. I didn't care. I had to get to my mom.

• • •

I got there in record time. The lights were on. I looked inside and didn't see anyone. I pushed open the door and ran inside. My mom was in the kitchen, trying to get the phone to work. I breathed a sigh of relief. "Are you okay?"

"I'm fine. The phones are out. Why didn't you come home earlier?"

"For what?"

"It's a blizzard out there, Ryan! Didn't you notice? The forecast says it's going to get worse. Frozen rain, sleet, hail—it's dangerous. They're telling everyone to take cover. We're going into the basement. Come on."

"I can't," I said, still out of breath.

"What?"

"I have to go back."

"No, you're not."

"I have to tell the others. They'll stay out there. I need to go get 'em."

"They don't have enough sense to go home themselves?"

"Not right now, they don't. Can I go?"

"Okay. But you make sure you're back in this house in five minutes. I'll call some of the other parents if I can get the phone to work."

"Got it."

I was out the door before I could take another breath.

TEN

THE BRIDGE

THE STORM HAD GOTTEN EVEN worse since I'd left just 10 minutes before. Visibility was down to about 30 feet. I couldn't even see the creek, much less the people on the other side of it. None of our troops appeared to have moved from their stations. Nelson was still in his tree; everyone else was in their crouched positions. They were going through with this, no matter what.

I shouted, "Go home! There's a storm coming!" But no one listened. They were soldiers, protecting their land. If they left, the Maxites would destroy their houses without a fight. They could not back down now.

I ran to Alice. "Alice! Tell them to retreat. We have to get out of here!"

"It's too late," she said. "I've already sent a Green Beret team out."

"What?"

"Three of our men snuck around the wall and are taking out the bridge at this very moment."

"What?!" The bridge was made out of heavy chains and

wooden slats, and it was fastened onto the bank with screws into wooden planks. A heavy-duty wrench could free the chains and drop the bridge into the water.

"No!" I yelled, running toward the creek. The Maxite army was marching double-file toward the bridge, their snowball bags at the ready. I plunged through the opening in the wall and saw that I was one moment too late. The first man was about to cross when—"Now!" I heard from below the bridge, and suddenly, the chains fell and the bridge collapsed into the rushing creek. Several pieces of wood broke in half on the rocks, destroying any chance of ever using the bridge again. The Maxite first in line nearly fell in, but then he found his balance and scrambled back onto the bank.

Max ran up to see what was happening and saw that there was no way for them to get across the creek. The water rushed past us, out of control and rising. To cross it on foot would be too dangerous in such a current.

The Green Beret team high-fived each other, but no one else found this very funny. The Maxites were in trouble. The driving ice and rain hurt our faces. We had to get these people to safety. No longer were these people our enemies, they were people in grave danger.

"How are we gonna get outta here?" a Maxite yelled.

Alice rushed up to me, realizing the same thing I did. We had to help them. "The rope!" she shouted. "I put a rope upstream. You can go across on that!"

"No," Max yelled. "We found that rope and cut it in half."

Nelson ran up. "Try this." He squeezed his Moccasin through the door in the wall.

We lowered the craft into the water, and Alice held it as steady as she could. There were launching ropes on both sides of the boat. People on either side could hold the ropes tight so the watercraft wouldn't get swept away in the current. Nelson and I held one end, and a couple of Maxites held the other end.

Slowly, the first two Maxites got into the boat. Their weight, plus the current, made holding onto the rope difficult. With all the strength we had, we pulled them across and they stepped onto the bank.

Hey, this was working! A crowd of Kidsborians had gathered on the banks and were clapping.

The Moccasin threatened to get away from us in the swift current, and the Maxites on the other shore started to panic. Four of them scrambled to get on at once.

"No! Two at a time!" Nelson shouted. The four fought each other to make room, and the weight was enormous. Mark came up behind us to help pull them in, but it was too much.

The boat capsized, sending all four into the water. Two of them leaped onto the shore, but two more were caught by the current. I let go of the rope and jumped into the freezing water. Alice jumped in after me. I grabbed hold of a hand—I'm not sure whose—and battled the current, but it was too strong. Nelson had my feet. The water was pouring over my face, but I briefly saw that Alice had rescued one person, and she was coming after me. I felt a strong arm grasp under my arms and pull me onto the bank. The boy I tried to rescue was on the shore with me. We all watched as the Moccasin was taken by the current. It plummeted down the waterfall.

I turned to anyone who was listening. "Run to Whit's End! Get Mr. Whittaker! And call the fire department!"

But the fire department was 10 minutes away, and with the roads as icy as they were, it might even take 20. These people needed to get across now. But the fire department gave me an idea . . . fire truck . . . ladder . . .

"The wall!" I shouted, rising to my feet. "We'll take down the wall and lay it across. They can crawl across it."

Everyone seemed to like this idea, or at least they weren't sure they could come up with anything else, so we scrambled to the wall. Alice knocked it down with one heave, and 10 of us picked it up and took it to the edge of the creek. Slowly, we inched it across, until it made a bridge.

The first Maxite, Luke Antonelli, tried it out. Before he ventured across, he pounded the wood into the ground on the other bank. He was trying to make sure it was sturdy. It wasn't. Max had obviously built a shoddy wall. Luke inched across one wooden plank, but it cracked in the middle. He backed off and tried another one.

Three planks later, he found one that held. But he had to take it slowly. He shifted to place some of his weight on a wire that stretched across. If this piece of wood broke, the wall would be worthless.

Everyone on both sides of the creek held their breath as Luke inched like a caterpillar across the makeshift bridge. I reached out my hand for him, and he stuck out his own. We connected, and three of us pulled him across.

The next Maxite was ready, and with more confidence after seeing it done, he crawled more quickly.

With every person, the wood seemed to groan a little more. Finally, it was Max's turn, the last Maxite to go.

He started across. The wood creaked. Panicking, he burst forward.

Too fast.

The wood cracked, bent, and shattered underneath him. As he fell toward the water, he flung out his hand—and found mine. I grasped with all my might and held him for a split second until I felt a strong hand reach across me and grab Max's wrist. It was Mr. Whittaker.

Max dangled from his hand for a moment, then with one big heave, we pulled him ashore.

We caught our breath, and then we all ran through Kidsboro toward Whit's End.

• • •

Most of the people ran on to their own homes, but some went to Whit's End because it was closer. Five Maxites and four Kidsborians took shelter under its roof. Mr. Whittaker called everybody's parents to tell them we were okay and would be welcome to stay until the storm passed. Two of the people who had to stay were Max and Scott. Max never said thank you, but he nodded to me once, and that was enough. I could expect no more from him.

Mr. Whittaker had some clean clothes he kept on hand for Little Theater productions. I chose some clothes like Joseph from the Christmas story. I put them on and sat in front of the fireplace. I saw Scott on my way from the bathroom, and he smiled at me and said, "So, you think you're Aquaman now?"

I smiled back and said, "Pretty much."

Mr. Whittaker ran around serving everyone hot chocolate. I took a cup and said, "Thank you." Our eyes met.

"I'm sorry, Mr. Whittaker. I was mad at you, and you were just trying to teach me something."

"That's okay, Ryan. Sometimes people pay a price to learn a lesson, and sometimes people pay a price to teach one. The important thing is that the lesson was learned."

"Yeah. I guess so."

"Merry Christmas, Ryan," he said.

"Merry Christmas, Mr. Whittaker."

It was the eve of Christmas Eve, and for the first time, it felt like it. There was peace inside Whit's End. There was a nativity scene on the mantle above the fireplace. I moved one of the shepherds so that he could clearly see the baby Jesus. Scott did the same for a donkey.

The smiles all around and Christmas decorations made it seem like a party. Imagine that—mortal enemies having a party together.

• • •

The storm lasted through the night, and we all slept at Whit's End. No one seemed to mind. When morning broke, a bunch of us, both Kidsborians and Maxites, trudged through the two feet of new snow toward our clubhouses.

The wall was still there, except it was no longer dividing our two cities. Instead, it was the bridge between them. The first thing Max did was start tearing down the rest of the wall. Since he had been too proud the night before to thank me for saving his life, I figured this was his way of saying that the days of two separate nations were over. Kidsboro and Bettertown would live on as cities of peace. The other three Maxites helped him.

Scott stayed behind in Kidsboro, which was half buried in snow. The icy rain had fused our arsenal of snowballs together, so now it was one big, solid mountain. They were never even used . . . until now.

Scott found a Kidsborian flag and pulled it out of the ground. He walked over to the mountain and began to climb it, all the way up, six feet high. He looked around at all the people watching him, and then he raised his hand and plunged the flagpole into the mountain. It stuck firm and waved majestically in the breeze.

We claim this land for Kidsboro.

THE END